Time In Space

Adora Hooper

ISBN: 0692339043
ISBN-13: 978-0692339046

DEDICATION

This book is dedicated to my Mom and to her mom,
Mom Dee. These two wonderful women in my life
taught me to follow my dreams. If it wasn't for
Mom's guidance and counsel, I would never have
made this book a reality. If it wasn't for Mom Dee
and Mom's combined enthusiasm for me to follow
my dreams, I never would have become the young
lady I am today. I love them both so much!

CONTENTS

ACKNOWLEDGMENTS

This book would have never been finished if it wasn't for all of the help, inspiration, and encouragement given to me by my friends and family. I'd like to mention a few of them: Dad, Poppy, Nanny, Papa, Dwayne, Rob, Busch, Heidi, David, Steven, Carol, Jeanne, Cliff, and Bob. I couldn't have finished this book so well without the patience shown to me as well as a ton of help from Dave, Patrick, Grizz, Jeff, Carolyn, and Mom.

PROLOGUE

Niemand groaned as he helped Deborah out of the wrecked spaceship. His leg hurt, but it wasn't anything compared to Deborah's injuries. She had a gaping cut on her forehead that was bleeding badly. He only hoped that the baby was alright as he gently set her down.

Deborah was of royal blood on the planet on which war had just come to. Her father, King Zonien, had entrusted Niemand to keep his daughter and grandchild safe as he was her personal pilot. He had tried his best, but a couple of small Nythian fighter ships had attacked them just as they jumped into hyperspace, critically damaging the ship. Despite the best efforts of the ship's Artificial Intelligence helping him stabilize its erratic flight path, they had had to make a very rough emergency landing on this remote, uncharted planet.

"Niemand?" The faint call came from Deborah's lips.

"I'm here, Your Highness." was his quick response as he took her hand.

"No formalities, Niemand, please." Deborah said softly. She had spent most of the trip in labor and they both knew that the baby would be born at any moment. He only wished he knew more about first aid as well as how to take care of a woman in labor. The next hour was stressful and memorable; giving birth weakened Deborah further. "Please take good care of my baby..." Deborah said faintly, looking pleadingly into Niemand's eyes.

"Deborah! You had twins!" he exclaimed. When there was no response from Deborah, he realized she was dead.

At last the two babies were safely wrapped in a bedcover Niemand had recovered from the ship. Both babies started to cry as Niemand sobbed at the loss of his Princess, friend, and confidante.

Niemand rummaged through the contents

of what had been the ship's food locker, searching frantically for something to feed the infants. Dried food packets littered the ground around the wreckage. But no milk. No formula. Nothing of use. He bellowed in frustration and the startled babes replied with cries of hunger.

A roar from overhead drowned out the newborns' hungry cries. Niemand watched as a small craft slowed its approach, hovered and landed near the wreckage. Having lost his blaster in the crash, he hoped it was a friendly vessel.

Three uniformed men came out carrying weapons but, to Niemand's relief, their attitude appeared more cautious than threatening. "Hello," one of them called as they approached. "Do you need help? What's your name?" they called from a short distance away.

"Hello. My name is Niemand and I do need help," he called back, addressing the man who had spoken. Niemand judged him to be the leader. "I have two baby girls here, their mother died in childbirth, and my ship is damaged. Can you give me a lift to another planet if I show you its location?"

The group came closer to investigate this lone man. They saw the two precious bundled up babies and their dead mother. "Are you the father?" The leader asked Niemand, suspicious of this strange man who had two babies and a dead woman with him.

"No, I was their mother's pilot. We were attacked and she was seriously injured when we crash landed. I need to get the babies back to their grandfather, King Zonien. He's the King of the Terbiates."

The leader then pulled a fist-sized communicator from his belt and, cueing the communicator, called "We have a damaged ship, two baby girls, a dead woman and a man who is requesting a lift back to an unknown planet controlled by an alien race called the 'Terbiates.' Permission requested to give them a lift."

The communicator came to life with a staticy hiss. "Permission granted."

"Please come with us," the leader of the team said with a grim smile as his two men each picked up a baby. "We'll send another team out here to collect your ship and the lady's remains."

"Thank you very much." Niemand replied as he followed them, all the while keeping a close eye on his two precious charges.

Once on board the ship, Niemand was assigned a room where he and the babies would stay. He was also supplied with two bottles of a nutritious formula to feed the babies. The two babies greedily consumed the warm milk as Niemand held the bottles. Once they were fed, the babies contentedly slept under Niemand's watchful gaze.

The Captain in charge of the ship had personally come down to bid him welcome and offer his condolences for what had happened to Deborah. With the Captain had come a beautiful lady in a similar uniform. The Captain introduced her as his first officer, Commander Sarah. She had a great big smile when she saw the twin girls and had cuddled with them under Niemand's piercing gaze.

Niemand was questioned by the Captain who asked who he was, who the babies were, who their mother had been, and about their history. Niemand told the Captain enough to satisfy him, but he kept the secret about the special genes that the two girls possessed. He was grateful to the Captain for the ride, but he would not trust the twins' biggest secret with anybody.

Niemand gave the Captain coordinates to his homeworld and was assured that it wouldn't take very long to get there - probably a day at most. Farewells had been exchanged and Niemand relaxed as he was left with his two new Princesses.

Niemand sighed as he thought about everything that had happened in the last few hours. He was having a hard time accepting that Princess Deborah was dead. He knew that he should stop thinking before he started crying. At least, they would be home very soon.

Looking around the room, Niemand spotted his cot and lay down after checking on the babies again. He was exhausted. He slowly closed his eyes and fell asleep almost instantly.

Niemand awoke to someone pinning him down on the cot. He struggled to get free. The two baby girls were crying! He felt a needle poke his arm and realized he was being drugged. Against his will, he slowly stopped fighting as he fell into sleep. His last thought was that he needed to make sure the girls were alright and that he was going to get even with whoever was behind this.

ॐ॰ॐ॰ॐ॰ॐ॰ॐ॰ॐ॰ॐ

Niemand was woken up by the Captain shaking his shoulder. "Get up, Niemand. This is where you get off."

Niemand jumped up. He remembered that the babies had been upset and crying. He glanced over at the bed where they had been laying last night. Only one baby was there!

"Where's the other baby?!" Niemand growled demandingly.

"You must be mistaken. There is only one baby." the Captain said coldly.

"I am not mistaken. I want the other Princess to be returned to me immediately." Niemand growled while taking a threatening step towards the Captain.

Two men raised their weapons and pointed them at Niemand. Niemand glanced at the guns and then retreated a step away from the Captain.

"I suggest you take your Princess and get off of my ship." the Captain coldly said. "You are no longer welcome here."

"You will not get away with kidnapping a royal Princess of the Terbiate people!" Niemand growled.

"It's your word against everyone else's word on this ship, Niemand. I wouldn't try to fight us if I were you." The Captain gave an icy smile. "Now, for the last time… *get off my ship.*"

Niemand wanted to fight them, but he could see that there was no chance he could do anything except get himself killed. He finally picked up the remaining Princess and let the guards escort him off of the ship.

❧❧❧❧❧❧

A few hours later, Niemand faced King Zonien. "It's good to see you again my friend!" King Zonien said warmly. "I trust that my daughter is safely hidden away?"

Niemand looked down before looking King Zonien in the eyes. "I'm afraid that my ship was damaged and crashed on a planet not far from here." He paused as everyone in the court gasped. "Princess Deborah, your daughter, gave birth to twin girls before she died."

Another gasp was followed by deathly silence. King Zonien broke the silence with a sob. "My little girl, my precious baby is dead?" he wailed tearfully.

"I'm sorry." Niemand quietly said as tears started to roll down his cheeks.

A few minutes later, King Zonien spoke

again. "What about her babies? Where are they?"

Niemand motioned for a nurse to bring out the baby he had carried into the city from the out-skirting landing pad where he had been dropped off. "The ship was damaged beyond repair. I had to hitch a ride home with people from Earth. While we were aboard, the Captain kidnapped the other baby.

The court gasped again. "He did what?!" King Zonien yelled. "They will not get away with this! Guards, get the Captain of the Earth vessel on the communicator and get my other grand-daughter back here!"

The young Princess started to cry because of the yelling and King Zonien stopped shouting. "Give her to me." he said quietly as a couple of the palace guards rushed away.

King Zonien started crying again as he held his precious grand-daughter close. He finally gave her back to the nurse. "Make sure arrangements are made for her care and make sure that she gets the best care ever!" He ordered.

"As you wish, King Zonien." the nurse replied and hurried away.

"As for you, Niemand…" King Zonien glared at the Princess's pilot who had returned with the news that his only child was dead.

Niemand gulped. He didn't like the glare that King Zonien was sending his way. He hoped that the King would still be rational, but he didn't want to insult him further. He lowered his eyes and said, "Yes, my King?"

"You come back with only one of my grand-daughters after unsatisfactorily piloting the ship that my daughter was on. You killed my daughter by letting that ship crash!" King Zonien raged.

Niemand flinched at the tone that the King was using with him. So much for rational. He gave a sigh of relief when the guards hurried back into the room and quietly consulted with the King. Maybe the King's wrath would fall on those who deserved it instead of on him.

"They found what?!" The King's voice rose an octave higher. The guard started to repeat himself, but King Zonien interrupted with a very cold voice. "I heard you. You are dismissed."

Niemand glanced up to see the King's angry eyes glaring at him. "Niemand. According to the captain of the vessel from Earth, you had killed one of the babies and hidden it in the sand. His team found it when they came back for my daughter's body."

"I did no such thing!" Niemand yelled,

shocked at the outrageous lie. "I would never hurt anyone of the royal blood!"

"Yet you did. Since my daughter cared so much for you, I won't execute you like you deserve for killing her and murdering one of my grand-daughters. You are to be locked up until further notice."

"But I didn't do anything of the sort!" Niemand pleaded with tears in his eyes.

"Take him away!" King Zonien growled.

Niemand was pulled away as he tried to plead his innocence. One of the guards hit Niemand in the stomach when he continued to talk. "Silence." the guard growled.

Niemand was silent for the rest of the way to the cell that he knew was to be his for a very long time. His face was wet with tears. How could King Zonien think that he would deliberately murder Princess Deborah and one of her babies?

He lay down on the cot in the cell and cried himself to sleep. Sleep was far from restful though as nightmares pressed him. Many times that night he woke with sobs of the pain he felt.

By the end of the night he had promised himself that he would find a way to escape from this cell and find that baby Princess. He would find her, bring her back to her home, and prove that he didn't spill the royal blood. The real question was how to get out.

A few days later on Earth, the Captain handed the baby girl over to Doctor White. "You are free to do with her as you want for a year, but then she needs to be given to a foster family until she is grown. This is our only living specimen of an alien, so don't kill it."

"Thank you sir. We'll take good care of this little baby specimen." Doctor White said with a cunning smile.

A little over a year later the couple who had been waiting for their new child were signing all of the disclaimers and release forms. Finally the papers were all signed and the child's accompanying nurse handed over the baby and left the couple and child with the Captain and Doctor White.

"You do understand that everything we tell you in here is to be kept absolutely confidential?" the Captain said, asking the young couple to verify the agreement.

"Yes, we understand completely and will never tell anyone else. You have our word!" the man responded as his wife nodded in agreement.

"You tell them Dr. White." The Captain said.

"The baby girl you now hold, Mrs. Cooper, is an alien. The Captain here negotiated for it during a peace treaty signing. We don't know how much she will change as she grows up, but she will need regular appointments with me for checkups." Dr. White explained. "We want to monitor her progress and see what exactly she becomes."

The shocked couple turned to the Captain who nodded his head in affirmation. "I don't really know what to say." Mr. Cooper finally said.

"It's okay. We know this is a big shock to you, Mr. and Mrs. Cooper. If you need us at any time, don't hesitate to call." The Captain smiled a little, trying to make this young couple feel a little bit better.

"Yes, you can call us at any time." Doctor White agreed. "We do need to know what you are going to name her right now though."

"Cindy D. Cooper." Mrs. Cooper replied without hesitation, looking lovingly down at her new baby. It didn't matter if this child was an alien or not, she still had the needs of any child and would be cared for as if she was their own.

"Good name." Dr. White replied. "Here is my card and the Captain's card. We will schedule monthly checkups for now."

"Thank you so very much for giving us this opportunity." Mr. Cooper said with a wide smile as he and his wife stood to leave. "We can't tell you how much this means to us."

CHAPTER 1

The forest was so quiet and peaceful as Cindy walked through it on her way home on the Northwest Coast of the United States. She was of an average height, had deep blue eyes, long, straight black hair and a ready smile. She was thirteen years old and would turn fourteen within the month, just before graduating from junior high school. She was very happy with her life. As she walked, Cindy thought of her family, her mom and dad and her sister, Candy. She thought of her pets and smiled. She had a Golden Retriever, named Goldilocks, and a black and white cat, named Sweetheart. She loved her work at the local pet store, her studies and her status in life.

Suddenly, the ground began to shake and

rumble. Cindy hurried towards the sound to see what was going on. An enormous object sat in the middle of a nearby clearing and she gasped when she realized that the object was a spaceship. She didn't know how she knew it was a spaceship - she just knew. It appeared that no one was around, so she stayed to study it. It looked like a silver colored plane, almost as large as a big commercial jet but with the wings folded back along its sides. As she cautiously moved around the ship, looking for an entrance, a cold, metallic click broke the silence behind her.

"Either you slowly put your hands behind your head and then slowly, quietly turn around or I'll shoot you right now," a deep, gruff male voice said.

Cindy quickly calculated her chances of escape and survival. She didn't want to die – the thought of dying scared her. She didn't want to be kidnapped either – that thought scared her as well. Yet, she decided to allow herself to be kidnapped instead of killed, since it was the least scary choice of the two. Slowly putting her hands behind her head, she stayed perfectly quiet, waiting for the person behind her to make the next move.

"Now turn around," he said. Cindy turned and saw that she was facing a man about six feet tall, with brown hair, brown eyes and wearing a long, black robe with some kind of strange, metallic brown shoes and a shirt. He studied her, noting that she wore blue jeans, a teal shirt, and a dark blue jacket. "What's your name?" he asked her.

"Why should I tell you?" Cindy asked with a slight hint of curiosity which overlaid her nervousness with a rebellious feeling. "For one I don't know your name and by the way what are you doing with a spaceship anyway?"

"How do you know it's a spaceship, Miss whoever you are?" he asked with a slight glare at her and a tone that said he wasn't amused.

"So I'm right!!" Cindy exclaimed with a satisfied grin. "How did you get it?" She was very interested now, having lost all of her nervousness, and she started to lower her hands. But when the mysterious stranger shook his head slightly, she thought better of it. "So what are you going to do with me?"

"I'm still thinking about that. Be quiet for a while so that I can think," the man said while Cindy rolled her eyes at him.

This guy has no clue, she thought, *Whoa, where has my cautious nature gone to? I should be scared right now. But I'm not – very interesting indeed.* She was quiet however as she reflected on why she wasn't scared any more. The man looked at

17

her considering his options.

"Okay, will you come with me willingly or do I have to force you?" The stranger had evidently reached a decision about her.

"I'll come willingly I suppose," Cindy said; but, as the man put his gun back in its holster, she ran as fast as she could, away from the ship, back toward the forest. As she reached the edge of the clearing, she heard a dinging sound – like a spoon striking a cup -, felt a slight shock and then slipped into unconsciousness.

The man walked up to Cindy shaking his head. "You shouldn't have tried running Miss." Gently picking her up, he walked into his ship. Once inside, he carried her down a narrow, brightly lit corridor to a doorway and opened it with a spoken command. There was a cot and a chest in one corner of the room. Walking to the other side of the room, he opened the door to an adjoining room.

Inside this room were boxes and crates with things he'd stored for emergency use. After carefully setting his unconscious burden down on the floor, he opened one of the boxes and pulled out a coil of rope, a blanket, and a pillow. "I'm sorry for doing this Miss, but it's for your own safety… and perhaps mine as well," he muttered as he tied Cindy's arms carefully - but very securely - behind her back. After he was sure that she wouldn't be able to untie the knot, he slipped the pillow under her head and covered her with the blanket to keep her from getting too cold.

After checking to be sure Cindy was still unconscious, the stranger walked out of the room and locked the door behind him. Going back into the glade, he rubbed out the footprints around the landing site, including those he and his prisoner had made while she was running away from him. There was nothing he could do about the damage caused by the ship, but he thought no-one was likely to know what had caused it.

It took a couple hours for the kidnapper to clean up anything and everything that might give a clue as to what had happened to Cindy. It was getting dark as he finished. Going back into his spaceship, he shut the outer hatch, took his seat in the cockpit and started up the engines. Warning lights flashed as he lifted off the ground. "Yes, I know what I'm doing is dangerous. Now shut up!" he growled, punching at each warning light with deliberation.

After climbing out of the planet's atmosphere, he plotted a jump point and activated the ship's autopilot. The jump drive immediately kicked in and, satisfied that the ship was on course, he retreated to his quarters, lowered the ambient lighting and flopped down on the cot. Trying to get to sleep was harder than he thought it would be. He kept worrying about the girl. Getting up, he went to her door, spoke the passcode and went into the room.

Good, she is still asleep, he thought. As he started to leave, something stopped him. Turning around, he kneeled down next to her and stroked her hair. "I hope that I'm doing the right thing Miss." His voice was soft and kind. Getting back up, he left the room, relocked the door with the code and went back to bed. As he drifted off to sleep, he mumbled, "I really hope this is the right thing to do."

A few hours later Cindy woke to find herself lying on a cold floor in the dark with a really bad headache. Her body ached so badly that she wasn't sure if she could get up. *What happened?* she wondered. Had she had been having a bad dream – or had it been real? If her brain would only wake up. But the more it woke up the more it told her that she had a huge headache.

It wasn't an easy task trying to make peace with her brain while, at the same time, trying to get up, but Cindy was giving it her best shot. She had to wake up, get rid of this headache, and find out why it was cold and dark. *Ohh… the power must be off.* she thought with a sigh. She relaxed under the cover and her eyelids slowly drifted shut again. Her last thoughts before surrendering to sleep were about her homework not being completed and how much trouble she would be in at school the next day.

Cindy groaned and rolled over. "It can't be morning yet," she mumbled as a bright light hit her eyelids. "Just a few more minutes of sleep, please."

"Sorry Miss, but you need to get up. I thought for sure that I had hit you with too big a stun bolt. Evidently you're pretty tough. I do know not to trust you though." The man sounded like he was trying to be serious… but failing miserably.

Cindy tried to push herself up with her arms and found them tied behind her back. *No wonder I'm sore*, she thought and then turned her head to look at the man who was standing over her. "What did you do to me? Where am I? Who are you? What are you planning to do with me? Why am I here?" The questions flew fast and furious to keep up with her temper as she kicked the blanket off.

"Easy Miss… don't go getting yourself all worked up. It'll be fine. But before we reach our destination I want to know a few things. You tell me who you are, how much you know about spaceships, and about other things in general. In return, I'll give you food, water, and take you to your home. Doesn't this sound fair?" he asked her in a calm, relaxed voice, raising his eyebrows in a questioning way.

"Okay. You add untying me to the deal, and I'll accept." Cindy glared at him – she was daring him to refuse – but to her surprise he reached down and cut the ropes without a word. "Thank you," she said sarcastically, sitting up to look around.

Spotting the open door, Cindy promptly jumped up and ran for it. As she was just about to go through the doorway, she hit an invisible barrier, bounced backwards, and collapsed.

The man just stayed put, a smile playing on his lips. Cindy scowled back at him. "That isn't funny," she said with a growl.

The man burst out laughing and when he was done, he said with a hint of admiration in his voice, "Well, I've got to admit, you do have a lot of spunk for a girl." An icy tone quickly replaced the admiration. "But listen here, Miss, I want to know who you are."

"Are you saying that you have no idea who I am?" Cindy asked with that annoying, bratty tone that always got her into trouble at home. Although, right now she didn't think she could be in any more trouble.

"Listen, Miss, this will be a lot easier if you trust me," the man said with a sigh. "Can't you please cooperate with me?"

"Umm… let me think… nope. I'm still not going to tell you anything. And trust?! You just kidnapped me. Do you really think that I'd trust you after that?" Cindy glared at him with anger rising in her chest. "You took me away from my family and life and you think that I'm going to be just fine? Well if that's what you think, you're dead wrong. You're a jerk and an idiot and I hate you!" She was screaming at him now while trying to keep her tears from spilling down her cheeks.

"I'm sorry, Miss, but I had to do it. You wouldn't understand if I told you why." The man walked out of the room and shut the door behind him. Leaning against it, he thought, *I've messed up big time.* He needed to get her back to where she belonged. Then maybe the pieces would start falling into place.

He walked to the control room and checked how much longer it would take for them to reach their destination. Nine hours. *How can I get her to believe the truth about herself, myself, and her past in less than nine hours?* he thought as he went back to his cot and lay down. *Well there's nothing I can do for the moment.* He closed his eyes, hoping to take a short nap.

Back in the room, Cindy was trying hard not to cry. She didn't want to cry. "I hate him. I hate him. I hate him!" she screamed at the walls and then broke down. "I don't hate him. I just want to go home." she said while trying to stop sobbing.

As the sobs subsided, she whispered the words to the wish that her Mom had taught her. "I wish I may, I wish I might, on the first star I see tonight that I could just go home." She burst into tears again because there was no star visible from her windowless compartment. She'd never get to go home again or see those she loved. She curled up into a ball and proceeded to cry herself to sleep.

CHAPTER 2

The man woke up an hour later and went to check on his passenger. Cautiously opening the door, he looked in. Seeing her curled up in a ball brought a sad smile to his face. Memories of before the Terbiate-Nythian war came into his mind, but he quickly banished them. There was no point in 'what ifs' or 'could've beens'. What was done was done and his Princess was dead. His dear Princess Deborah. But in her place, there was this pretty girl.

He walked over and knelt beside her. Looking at her tear streaked face deeply saddened him. He had made her cry. "If there is a god out there," he whispered as he wiped the dried tears off her cheeks, and if you are listening to me please, for her sake, make this worth her pain."

More than anything, he wanted to let the girl sleep. But he needed information before they reached their destination. Wiping all feelings from his face, he regretfully shook her awake.

When Cindy opened her eyes and saw who it was she immediately attacked him. He grabbed her arm and twisted it behind her back – not hard enough to hurt, but hard enough that she stayed put. "What do you want?" she demanded through gritted teeth.

"I want to know what your name is Miss." His voice was calm, but icy.

"I'm not going to ever tell you my name." Cindy said through her clenched teeth. She wanted to hurt this guy so badly, but she couldn't.

"Miss, we can do this the easy way or the hard way. You won't like the hard way, so I suggest that you cooperate." After a few tense moments with no answer from the girl, he twisted her arm just a little bit more.

"Ouch!"

"What is your name?" When she still didn't answer, he said, "Did you know that if twisted far enough a person's arm can be broken? Do you want that to happen to you?"

"No." Cindy forced through clenched

teeth. Her jaw ached from the strain. Her arm hurt. Her shoulder hurt. Her heart hurt. And there was nothing she could do about any of it.

"Okay then, tell me your name." He was trying to not allow his emotions to show, but he truly felt bad for it.

"My name . . . is none . . . of . . . your . . . business." Cindy growled out her reply as sweat started to bead on her forehead, but as soon as she did, her arm was twisted just a little bit farther. "Owww! It's Cindy. Cindy, Cindy, Cindy, I'm telling you it's Cindy!"

"That is much better Cindy." The man released her arm and she ran to the other end of the room.

"You're mean." Cindy yelled at him while cradling her hurt arm.

"That's what they all tell me," he said with a sigh. Sitting on one of the boxes, he added, "Cindy, I don't know if I'm in my right mind or not in telling you the truth. Your grandfather might like the honor of doing that himself. You obviously have no reason to trust me, but you are . . ." he paused and took a deep breath ". . . a Princess of the Terbiate people. People from Earth kidnapped you after they picked us up in a spacecraft. That was right after the spaceship I was flying crashed and your family were helplessly stranded on an unknown planet with me being unable to fix the craft." His eyes begged her to believe him. He hoped that she would trust him and accept that this little bit was true.

"After zapping me, kidnapping me and torturing me, you expect me to believe a story like that?! You're just a cruel, heartless, bully … and an idiot!" she sneered.

"Not only that, I have no idea who the Terbiate people are." Cindy paused and then continued. "I am not a Princess. I am a thirteen year old girl and I have little knowledge of how the world works or why people act as they do... especially you. I'm a student, as in someone who needs to be taught. Not someone who's a ruler." She took a step towards the man.

"You might not know a lot of things, but we'll teach you what you need to know Princess Cindy." His voice sounded a little bit excited. "You don't know how long it took me to figure out which planet you were located on. It has been a long twelve years since I was blamed for your disappearance. Since then, I've devoted myself to finding you and serving you as I served your mother."

"It took you twelve years to find out where

I was?" Cindy said skeptically. Not wanting to get within reach of him, she took a few steps backward.

"You may or may not know it, but your grandfather's kingdom includes several inhabited planets and there are many, many more in the galaxy. I had to search for a long time to find which planet you were taken to and then figure out how exactly to make you disappear." He got up and stepped towards her.

Cindy very quickly backed away. "I don't believe you. I don't trust you. Stay away from me." she said warily.

The man stepped back towards the door. "Okay, I'll show you what I'm talking about in about seven hours. Until then I'll leave you alone. If you want to talk to me here is a communicator." He laid a small, flat, rectangular object down on the floor and then turned to go. Before leaving the room, he looked over his shoulder at her and said, "Oh, by the way, my name is Niemand."

After Niemand left, closing and locking the door behind him, Cindy glared at where he had been. She didn't want to trust him, yet she was beginning to. *What if he was telling me the truth about my family?* She sat down on the floor, leaning against one of the boxes letting that big question and all its implications run through her head.

Directly outside the room, Niemand paused for a moment and thought, *Cindy. That is a nice name. I wonder who named her that?* He didn't like how his thoughts ended in a question. Questions were meant to be answered, but there was no way he could go back in there. Sighing, he returned to the cockpit and checked on their progress.

One of the warning lights on the center panel began to flash ominously. "What is it now?" he asked the ship's computer.

The computer verbally responded with, "We are currently low on fuel. The latest GPS update indicates a refueling station nearby. Should you bypass the station, calculations indicate the ship will run out of fuel prior to reaching another station."

"Then I guess we need to exit hyperspace and gas up," Niemand replied.

"It would be best to do so," the computer agreed. "But you need to give the order."

"I just did and if you don't start listening I'll put you in the scrap pile when we get home."

"Certainly, you are well within your rights to demand a computer upgrade. Nonetheless, no order was given to exit hyperspace and refuel. Nor has it been given yet."

Niemand sighed. The ship's computer was, like all computers, far too literal. "Maintain autopilot," he instructed. "When we're within range of the nearest refueling station, exit hyperspace and wake me. Until then, I'm going to take a nap." For now, there was nothing to do other than rest. He headed back to his quarters and laying down, closed his eyes, falling asleep almost instantly.

Back in the room Cindy had finally realized she needed more information before deciding if Niemand's story was, indeed, true. She stood up, walked over to the communicator, and picked it up. It fit well into her hand and had a single button in the center. She pushed the button and a computer-like voice responded immediately, "Yes?"

Startled, Cindy dropped the communicator. That wasn't Niemand's voice. Staring skeptically at it, she waited. Nothing happened, so she picked it back up, clutching it as if to choke the life from the voice within.

Pushing the button again, she said, "Niemand?"

"Niemand is unavailable at this time." replied the slightly nasal, matter-of-fact voice. "May I help you?"

"Who is this?"

"I am the ship's computerized control interface. If you like, you can call me Cosmos... although I should warn you that the current pilot of this vessel prefers to keep things on a purely business-like level. Nonetheless, I control the ship and all its functions whenever the pilot requires my assistance."

"Oh okay, Cosmos," Cindy said softly. "I was wondering where we are going."

"We are going to Terbite."

"Where is that compared to Earth?"

"Terbite's position in space, relative to Earth, is beyond practical description. It's position, relative to time, is approximately nine hours from Earth at the ship's maximum hyperspeed."

"Okay, do you know how much longer it will take until we get to Terbite?"

"If circumstances do not change, it will take eleven hours, ten minutes and forty-five seconds."

"But Niemand said that we were supposed

to get there in less than seven hours." Cindy said exasperated.

"Niemand probably didn't know that we needed to refuel when he told you that." Cosmos's voice came over the communicator in the same matter-of-fact tone as always.

"Oh okay." Cindy's voice relaxed, as did her strangle-hold grip on the communicator.

"Can I help you with anything else?" offered Cosmos.

Cindy smiled mischievously. "Would you mind opening the door for me?" she asked, assuming that the ship's computer was programmed to obey any command. She expected that Cosmos would open the door for her.

"I'm sorry, but I'm not allowed to open that door without the command code."

Cindy sighed. Of course, trust the bad guys to program the ship's interface so it requires a command code to unlock the door. Never mind something more complicated like ordering Cosmos to turn the ship around and take her back home. Why would she even think that they'd make it easy for her? She felt like banging her head against the bulkhead in frustration, but she had to focus on how to get out of here.

Suddenly there was a jolt throughout the

ship. Cindy lost her balance and hit the floor. "What happened?" she yelled into the communicator.

"We have dropped out of hyperspace."

"Really? Who's driving this thing? I could've been hurt."

"Perhaps I should have warned you. Evidently you have not gained your space legs yet. My apologies Miss. Are you injured?"

"It's okay. My name isn't 'Miss' – it is Cindy." Cindy sighed as she got back to her feet.

"I'll call you Cindy then if it is okay with you."

"Yeah, it's okay with me," Cindy said, but then thought, *Why am I talking to a computer ship interface?* She couldn't think of a good enough reason, so she set the communicator back down on the floor.

Sitting down with her back against one of the boxes, Cindy sighed. She wanted out of here. She wanted out of here now. She didn't even want to imagine being in here!

Sighing again, Cindy glared at the communicator. If she glared at it enough, maybe it would melt. She kept blinking and losing her focus so she gave up.

Cindy closed her eyes for a minute, but then quickly reopened them as the ship shuddered. Crawling forward, she picked up the communicator. "What is going on Cosmos?" she asked worriedly.

"We are being attacked. Please remain calm. Niemand will take care of this."

"We're being attacked and you want me to remain calm?!?" Cindy yelled and then ordered, "Let me out of this room . . . now."

"I'm sorry Cindy, but this is not a good time for a chat. Please stand by."

Cindy growled and staggered as the ship bucked again. She yelled into the communicator, "This isn't fair. Let me out of here right now!" She was thankful to hear Niemand's voice in reply.

"Cindy, just get down and stay down until I say otherwise. I can't help you right now and, at the moment, you're safer in there than you would be out here. You're going to have to trust me on this one." Niemand's voice was calming and reassuring.

Sighing, Cindy stayed on the floor, holding tightly to the communicator. The ship kept lurching and it made for a very uncomfortable ride.

After what seemed like hours, but really was only about ten minutes, Cindy heard Niemand's voice over the communicator. "Cindy, you need to trust me and do what I say right now, okay?"

Cindy pushed the button down and barely breathed the word "Okay."

The word must have been loud enough for Niemand to hear because he quickly continued. "Get to the door. I'll be there in a second. Hurry. We have to evacuate the ship."

Cindy got up and was thrown against the door as the ship was jarred once again. She remained there, leaning against the door, waiting patiently. Five minutes passed without a sound or a another jar. Ten minutes passed without anything happening.

Finally Cindy grew tired of waiting and spoke into the communicator. "Niemand, where are you? What's going on?"

There was no answer, but the door opened. A stranger stood in the corridor, blocking Cindy's way. She peered around him to catch a glimpse of two more men dragging Niemand out of sight.

"Who are you?" Cindy asked the stranger.

The stranger's only reply was to point a dagger shaped object at Cindy. There was a dinging sound and a green beam shot out from the end. As the beam hit her, she felt a slight shock and then slipped into unconsciousness. Again.

CHAPTER 3

Cindy woke up in a dark room. Her head hurt so badly! She grunted as she tried to sit up. It was hard since her hands were tied behind her back. Again. She eventually got her body into a kneeling position. She couldn't see anything. She tried to adjust her eyes, but there wasn't any light anywhere. She carefully stood up. Her body ached. *What did that guy do to me?* she wondered. Stepping forward, she promptly tripped over something.

"Ow!" A little voice said. "Could you please stay put?"

"What? Who are you?" Cindy asked, quickly sliding away. Her back touched a couple of bars and, when she got shocked, she jumped back about a foot.

"I'm your fellow captive." the quiet voice

said. "Don't worry, I won't eat you." The voice laughed.

"Where am I? And who are you?" Cindy asked.

"We are on a Nythian ship. My name is Daruka," the female voice replied.

Cindy was quiet for a minute and then asked, "What's going to happen to us, Daruka?"

"I'm not sure, but I'm guessing that they'll train us for use in the Terbiate-Nythian war." Daruka replied frankly.

"I see," Cindy said.

"Hold on, we're landing now." As Daruka spoke the spaceship hit something hard enough that Cindy lost her seat. A door banged open and Cindy was blinded by the light. When she regained her sight she saw Daruka being taken away by two men. The door closed, leaving her in total darkness.

A little while later, the door slammed open again and two more men came over and grabbed her. "Let me go!" Cindy yelled, but they ignored her. Instead, they half carried and half dragged a yelling and kicking Cindy out of the cell. From the corridor, the men took her to another room, well lit but sparsely furnished. When they finally put her down, she quickly moved away from them.

A gentle hand touched her shoulder and Cindy jumped, but her nerves settled down as a kind voice said. "Hello there. Don't be afraid. Come with me please."

Cindy turned around to see a woman that was old enough to be her grandmother smiling down at her. Glancing back over her shoulder, she noticed that the men were guarding the door – her only escape route – so she decided to follow the old woman.

The woman led Cindy to a pile of rugs in the far corner of the room, motioning for her to sit. Cindy sat and then watched her go over to talk to the guards. After they had conversed for a moment, the men left and she came back over to where Cindy quietly sat waiting.

"My name is Miarat, but you can call me Mia," she said in a pleasant voice.

"Hi," Cindy replied in a tone that was anything but nice.

"Okay, I'm sure that you want to know where you're at and what you are doing here. Am I right?" Mia said in the same pleasant voice.

"Yep," Cindy replied in a little bit nicer tone.

"As of now, you are in the first stages of training. You have been chosen to fight against the Terbiates along with other Nythian soldiers." Mia said in a matter-of-fact voice.

"Wait. That's not right. I was supposed to help the Terbiate people," Cindy thought out loud. "I was told that I'm a Terbiate princess." The only thing that that statement got her was a slap. "Ouch! What was that for?"

"My apologies Cindy. I shouldn't have hit you. I don't want you to ever even think about helping the Terbiates. They are evil." Mia said coldly.

"Hmmm…," was Cindy's reply. "What am I going to be trained to do?"

"For now, in step one of your training process, you will be taught how to read and write the Nythiash language fluently." Mia answered. "Now I have a question for you: what is your name?"

"You probably already know my name, don't you?" Cindy retorted.

"Yes, I do, but I'd like you to tell me willingly," Mia explained.

"Fine, it's Cindy," Cindy said icily.

"It is nice to meet you Cindy." Mia smiled.

"Yeah, right." Cindy looked away, fixating on the closed door.

"You'd better get used to having me around. I'm the only person that you will be seeing for the next month." Mia grinned as

Cindy jerked her head back around with a very surprised look on her face.

"Okay…" Cindy dragged the word out while thinking about what Mia had just said. After finding no immediate reply to Mia's statement, she asked "What happened to Niemand?"

"Niemand? Who is that?" Mia asked, puzzled.

"Niemand is the man who was with me when your people captured us," Cindy tried to explain.

"I wasn't aware that you were brought in with anyone." Mia said.

"Oh okay," Cindy sighed.

"I can try to find out if you want me to," Mia said in a cheerful tone.

"I'd like that. Thanks." Cindy gave Mia a slight, quick smile.

"You're welcome. Now it is time for sleep. Tomorrow will come sooner than you like." Mia smiled. "You will sleep here and I'll be over by the door. If you need to refresh yourself, the button over there…," she motioned to a small, square, yellowish button on the opposite wall, "will open a door to an alcove built for that purpose."

"Okay. Thank you," Cindy quietly said, then yawned and lay down, pulling some of the rugs over her.

Mia said, "Good night Cindy." But Cindy, exhausted by the events of the last few days, was already asleep.

When Cindy opened her eyes the next morning she took in her surroundings slowly and carefully. She knew that she couldn't afford to overlook any possible way of escape – her first and foremost goal was to get back home to Earth. "Maybe I can steal a spaceship," she thought.

Dull gray light shone meekly through a couple of windows far above eye level on the wall opposite Mia's bed showing that the room was bare and empty except for the door to the alcove, the open doorway leading outside, her bed, and Mia's bed.

There was no sign of Mia. Cindy decided to see what was outside of the room. Stepping to the doorway and pulling aside the curtain, she looked out. There was a rotunda with many other doorways like hers with colorful curtains used as doors, but she decided to not venture out as there were quite a few guards stationed around the rotunda.

Going back to her sleeping area, Cindy

straightened the rugs and then quietly sat waiting for Mia to come back. She knew that she had to be patient so, to pass the time, Cindy twiddled her thumbs. After a while, she was working all eight fingers. She was starting to think about twiddling her toes as well when Mia came through the doorway carrying a basket. Cindy spoke rapidly. "Where were you? What are we going to do today? Is there anything to eat? Can I go outside? What's in the basket?"

Mia quietly laughed and then answered Cindy's rapid questions with slow answers as she set her basket down on the ground. "I was getting your studies for the day and breakfast for us. I am going to teach you how to read and write some of the Nythiash alphabet and language. Yes, I brought food for breakfast – figs, bread, raisins, and grapes. No, you have to stay in this room. The items in the basket are the supplies for today."

Cindy giggled. "How did you remember and understand all of my questions?"

"When you get as old as I am and have had as much practice as I have, it becomes second nature." Mia smiled at Cindy. "I'm glad you are more cheerful this morning than you were last night. Now let's have some breakfast, okay?"

"Okay." Cindy agreed with an eager nod.

Mia dug two plates and a couple of boxes of fruit out of the basket. This she dumped on the plates, added a couple pieces of bread, then handed one of the plates to Cindy who was eagerly waiting to eat.

Cindy waited until Mia had taken a bite of her bread before trying her own. It tasted sweet. Cindy grinned at Mia and commented, "It's good. Thanks."

Mia smiled and continued her breakfast. Cindy followed her example and quickly ate the bread and fruit that was on her plate. The figs, grapes, and bread were the best – she didn't really like the texture of the raisins, but it all tasted pretty good. She was also hungry and when a growing teenager is hungry, almost anything tastes good!

Cindy handed her plate to Mia when asked and then waited for what would come next. Mia dug a book and something shaped like an old fashioned chalkboard out of the basket. "What's that?" Cindy asked, curious about the object.

"This is a writing board." Mia replied.

"Okay." Cindy nodded in understanding. *So that's a writing board*, she thought. *I can remember that.*

"You use the writing board by placing it on

your lap and using your finger to write," Mia explained and then showed Cindy what she meant. "You try it now," she said as she handed it to Cindy.

Cindy ran her finger over the writing board after setting it on her lap. The writing board responded quite well to her light touch. She wrote one single sentence on the board. It read: I miss home. "How do I erase it now?" she asked Mia as she wiped a tear out of the corner of her eye.

"Just push this button." Mia showed her a small button on the top right corner of the device and then squeezed her shoulder. "It will be okay Cindy."

Cindy looked at Mia in astonishment. "You could read what I wrote?"

"No, but I'm guessing it had something to do with your home by the tear you wiped away," Mia said quietly.

"Well… you were right," Cindy replied and then asked, "So what do I do now?"

Mia showed Cindy how to form the first several letters of the Nythiash alphabet and then left her to practice. Satisfied, Mia then pulled out some coarse, thick thread from the basket and busied her own hands and mind with weaving the thread into a patch of cloth. Occasional glances at Cindy's work convinced

Mia that her student was a quick learner.

At lunch time Mia said with a smile, "You are a good student and are making great progress!"

"Thanks," Cindy grinned back.

Lunch consisted of more bread only this time it had a coating of something sweet and gooey. After questioning Mia about the coating, Cindy learned that it was like a jam. It made the bread taste even better and Cindy greatly enjoyed the meal.

After lunch, Cindy went back to work on her lessons, copying new letters from the book Mia had given her. She wanted to learn the entire Nythiash alphabet in one day, but, halfway through the book, Mia finally said, "Okay, it's time to be done with studies for now. You did very well!" She smiled.

Mia packed everything away in the basket, brought out a couple boxes of fruit and handed one to Cindy. Cindy took it and savored the flavor of the grapes, figs, and raisins.

When they were done with their last meal of the day, Mia packed the empty fruit boxes back into the basket, exchanged "Good night's" with Cindy, and then left with the basket. Cindy watched her go then curled up on her rug and fell asleep almost immediately.

A little while later, Mia came back into the room, without the basket, laid down on her own rug and slept.

⁂

The next day consisted of the same schedule, only Mia brought news.

"Your friend, Niemand, is doing well," she said with a small smile at Cindy. "He is being trained, like you are, only in different things since he knows more than you do about Nythians."

"Okay. I'm glad he is doing well. Thanks for finding out for me." Cindy smiled back at Mia.

"You are welcome. Now let's get back to work on the Nythiash alphabet, shall we?"

Cindy groaned a little bit, but the smile on her face said that she didn't mind the work. "Sure," was her reply as she got back to work on learning the language.

CHAPTER 4

For the next several weeks, the only change was the amount of knowledge that Cindy was storing in her head about reading, writing and speaking the Nythiash language.

As Cindy was a very quick learner, she could read and write anything in the Nythiash language very quickly and effectively by the end of four weeks. Mia announced that she was ready for step two in her training.

The night when Cindy saw Mia for the last time, Cindy hugged her. "Thank you for everything," she said.

"You are very welcome. Take care of yourself," Mia replied with a hug of her own. They then exchanged good night's and went to sleep, just like any other night, only Cindy knew that this had been the last day with Mia.

ষ্টৃৎষ্টৃৎষ্টৃৎৎষ্টৃৎৎষ্টৃৎ

When Cindy woke up the next day, she looked at Mia's bed, sort of hoping that she would be still there. She wasn't. Cindy sighed. There was a part of her that had grown somewhat attached to Mia and that part was sad at the prospect of never seeing Mia again.

After Cindy made her bed, she awaited developments. A guard appeared in the doorway with a jerk of his arm to pull the curtain aside and motioned for Cindy to follow him. Cindy got up and quietly followed him to a building with long rows of bunk beds.

Cindy looked at them in wonder. *What was this place? And what am I doing here?* she wondered as she took a careful look around her. The guard left without a word while Cindy watched silently as many other girls marched in single file into the building.

The girls broke out of formation and went to beds that apparently belonged to them. Cindy wasn't sure what to do, but she decided to walk along the rows trying to find one for her own.

Some of the girls pretended that they didn't see Cindy, others hissed insults at her, and still others pushed her as she walked past them.

Cindy finally found a bunk that was unoccupied. The girl that had the bottom bed didn't seem too bad – she didn't smile at Cindy, but she didn't push or hiss insults at her either.

Cindy decided to try talking to the girl. "Hi. I'm Cindy. What's your name?"

The only response Cindy got was a glare. She sighed. *Oh well… I tried.* she thought as she climbed up onto the top bunk. She wondered a little bit about what was going to happen, but not too much.

After Cindy spent some time just sitting on the bed, laying down on it, getting back up, and being completely bored, a woman came in. All of the girls stood at attention like Cindy had seen in movies about military schools back home on Earth.

Cindy's brain began to piece together what was happening to her. *The Nythians really are training me to be a soldier?!* The thought scared her a bit – she wasn't a soldier. She didn't like the thought of hurting anyone – well, other than Niemand – there were plenty of things she would like to do to him for getting her into this mess!

As Cindy's mind was trying to formulate a plan to get out of this very unpleasant situation, the woman came up and stood right in front of her. Cindy jumped with shock as the woman's voice snapped Cindy's thoughts back from her planning as she said, "Cindy … Attention!"

After getting over her first scare though, she scowled at the woman, crossed her arms, and proceeded to glare at her while slouching just a little bit. It was her favorite posture for use on her teachers back home on Earth. Wait. She wasn't supposed to think about home. It made her somewhat sad, but not for long.

The woman's expression of disbelief, anger, and astonishment made Cindy double over laughing. Even some of the other kids giggled at the look on their Commander's face. With her face bright red from laughing so hard, Cindy stood awaiting her punishment. She knew that to keep order the woman would have to do something, but it was well worth any punishment in her opinion to have seen the look on the Commander's face.

"You, Miss Cindy," the Commander finally growled, "are going to help out in the scrap yard. What you did was most unwise."

"Yes ma'am." Cindy saluted mockingly with a twinkle in her eye. *What kind of cool things will I learn in the scrap yard?* She let her mind wander over the possibilities of what she could learn. *The more I learn, the sooner I'll be on my way back home. Now that was a good thought! I must hold onto it.*

"Hmm... maybe being part of the scrap yard is too good for you." The Commander glared at Cindy's mischievous smile and looked quite annoyed when she saw the twinkle in her newest recruit's eyes.

The other girls, however, found it quite entertaining to watch Cindy challenge the Commander's authority. As long as it didn't land them in trouble of course! Trouble for them would never do, but it was always fun to watch the new girl or, even better, girls learn the hard way not to mess with the Commander.

They were surprised when Cindy replied "Oh no, I don't think being part of the scrap yard is too good for me, but don't you think I might get into a little bit of trouble?" The mischievous smile grew larger.

"Just get your work done on time." The Commander growled and then stalked away. The other girls giggled at Cindy's mock salute behind their Commander's back. After the

Commander left, many of the girls crowded around her and asked questions about where she was from, what she knew, and other things. She answered their questions as best as she could without giving away too much information.

There was one girl though that Cindy was interested in. The girl just sat on her bed, didn't look around, and didn't talk to anyone. After a while the other kids finally decided to leave her alone and she saw her chance to meet the girl.

Cindy walked over and sat down on the bed next to the girl. "Hello?"

The girl turned her head and looked up at Cindy. "Hello Cindy."

Cindy gasped. "Daruka?!?"

"Yes, it's me. It has been a while; I'm really surprised that you remember the sound of my voice."

"I remember voices for a long time. How've you been?"

"Alright. I'm planning my escape – this is not where I belong. Most of these Nythians grew up in the military. I grew up on a farm, but there was a draft and I was forced to come here. I hate it! What are you planning on doing? Do you know what you've got yourself into?"

"Not sure exactly, no, but it can't be too bad, right?"

"It can be much worse than you think. Scrap duty is the hardest job out there. You'll be hauling junk and sorting the scrap into stuff that's worth reusing from the stuff that will just be melted down. The pieces of metal are heavy and I'm not sure that you're strong enough to haul it. Between that and the military training, you're going to be miserable!" Daruka predicted gloomily.

"Oh." was Cindy's only response as she put her chin in her hands and rested her elbows on her knees. The sigh that followed was both sad and frustrated.

"Don't worry about it. I'll keep an eye on you and when I get to finally go back home, I'll try to take you with me." Daruka said as she rubbed Cindy's back to let her know it would be okay.

"Thanks." Cindy attempted a smile at Daruka. "I just wish I wasn't so stupid" She pulled a face. "crossing the Commander first chance I get."

Daruka giggled. "It was funny though! Besides, you're strong on the inside and smart. Most kids would have already been killed, but you've shown the Nythians that you can learn quickly. Just keep doing that."

"Okay." Cindy managed a better smile for Daruka. "I'll do my best."

"Good. That's all anyone can ask for. Now, let's get some rest. You'll need it for tomorrow." Daruka laid down. "Good night, Cindy."

"Good night, Daruka." Cindy got up and walked back to her bunk and climbed up onto it. She laid down and looked up at the gray ceiling as the light faded. "I will not forget my mission – I will get back home to Earth . . . I will!"

For the first time in about a month, Cindy let her thoughts wander back to memories of home. She surprised herself a little while later with the realization that she hadn't cried this time. Yes, she still missed her family and life, but right now she needed to focus on how to get through this and how to get home. With that, she closed her eyes and fell into a peaceful sleep.

❧❧❧❧❧❧❧

The next morning Cindy was awakened by a loud voice yelling over what seemed to be a loudspeaker, "Get up! Move out in five!" Groggily she sat up, got off of the bed, and then got jostled into line by the other girls.

Marching along with other girls wasn't easy for Cindy. She was new to this and still half-asleep, but she made it just fine out to the training field where they were headed. Once she had woken up more, she decided that marching around the field wasn't so bad. The worst part about marching was that she was starving and her stomach kept growling!

Another girl named Vincah told Cindy with an understanding face that she had missed dinner the previous night, but that breakfast would be soon. Cindy smiled her thanks for this welcome news.

After they had done the morning marches, as Vincah had called them, they were able to sit down to a light breakfast of porridge. Cindy did not like the taste of this new food at all, but after Daruka showed her how to empty a packet stuck to the bottom of the bowl into the porridge, Cindy decided that her breakfast was okay after all. Once they had finished breakfast, the girls were shown to the showering facilities and told that every evening they would shower and change into fresh uniforms.

By the time they got done with military exercises and learning how to be effective in combat it was about noon. Cindy was worn out and sore from where the 'practice weapons' had hit her. They didn't leave you unconscious like the dagger things did, but they did leave you gasping for breath when the beam hit you!

As Cindy ate her simple lunch of bread and a soup that she guessed was something like tomato, she wondered what would happen next. She watched Daruka walk towards her and wondered how much information her friend would be able to give her on what to expect.

Daruka sat down next to Cindy and asked, "How are you holding up?"

Cindy looked at Daruka and replied, "I'm a little sore and tired, but I'm doing alright. How are you?"

"I'm fine." was the short reply.

Cindy decided that Daruka wasn't the chatty type so she was going to have to ask about whatever she happened to be curious about. "Daruka, what are we supposed to do after this break?"

"You are supposed to go to the scrap yard and work. I'm to report to the information center to answer questions about the farmers and how well the local farms are producing." Daruka sighed as she finished talking.

"Oh, okay." Cindy fell silent.

"We need to get to work now, Cindy."

Daruka said after a few moments of silence. She gestured to a tall man coming through the gate. "That's who you need to report to – he oversees the scrap yard work and workers."

Cindy got up, told Daruka farewell for the time being, then jogged over to the man. "Hi, my name is Cindy and I'm supposed to be working in the scrap yard." she said quickly.

The man turned and looked at her. "Hello there Cindy. My name is Articimus, but you can call me Art." His smile made her smile in return without really meaning to. "I'm going to guess that you've never really worked with scrap metal before?"

"You guess correctly, Art."

"Okay, then I'll go a little bit easy on you. Let's go." He turned and walked away with Cindy following him.

Art led Cindy to a building that had piles and piles of junk metal. "This is where you're going to work." he told her and showed her how to sort the metal. Strong metal good for building spaceship hulls and armor went in one pile; other types that had electronic parts mixed in went into another pile.

As Cindy began sorting, she wondered what kinds of electronics she was pulling out. She couldn't tell what each piece was or what it was used for though, so she'd have to wait to carry out the newest plan that was already forming in her mind.

Cindy worked until the sun was almost down behind a mountain. Art then helped her find her way back to the barracks in time for a dinner of bread and jam. She was happy because he'd told her that she was one of the best workers that he had. She laid down on her bed and was asleep almost before her head hit the pillow.

CHAPTER 5

Every day for the next two weeks, Cindy's schedule followed the same pattern. Military training in the morning … scrap sorting all afternoon and evening. The only difference was that the more she practiced, the fewer times she was hit with that awful beam. She could now keep up with Michella, another girl she had gotten to know fairly well, against a couple other girls-in-training.

Cindy's job at the scrap yard got better and better too. As she got stronger, Art assigned her more jobs. Today was the day that he said he'd have a surprise for her, so she found herself hurrying to the scrap yard after lunch break in anticipation.

Art met Cindy near where she usually worked. "Good afternoon, Cindy!" he exclaimed enthusiastically.

"Good afternoon, Art!" Cindy replied with even more enthusiasm than usual. She could hardly wait to see what the surprise was!

"Please, come with me." Art motioned Cindy to follow him to a different part of the scrap yard. It was at the area of the scrap yard where people analyzed the electronic parts that he stopped. "This is where you'll be working now." He pointed out another girl as he spoke. "Her name is Carla. She'll teach you what you need to know."

Cindy barely got out a "Thank you, Art." as he quickly walked away. She walked over to Carla. "Hi, my name is Cindy and Art said that I was supposed to learn from you?" her statement ended in a question bringing Carla's eyebrows up.

"Hi Cindy. I'm sure Art told you my name, but if he didn't, my name is Carla. And you are the first person that I've ever met to end a statement with a question without changing sentences." Carla's smile caused Cindy to smile as well.

"Hi Carla. I just do that sometimes, I don't know why." Cindy paused and then glanced at the ground. "I hope you don't mind."

Carla laughed. "No, I don't mind at all! But we've been talking enough about this, let's get some work done!"

Cindy grinned. "Okay!"

For the next couple of hours, Cindy learned how to recognize different ship components and what they did. There were components that took ships of different sizes into hyperspace, others that would use an energy beam to transfer physical objects onto and off of ships, weapon modules for different types of ships, and ship computer interfaces. The ship computer interfaces intrigued her. She wanted to have one to work with, but Carla said that the workers were never allowed to have any of the parts.

Cindy did her work well and learned quickly. Carla was impressed with her new partner. "You did very well, Cindy!" she said at the end of the day. "You'll one day be better than I am at this."

Cindy shook her head. "No - you are great at this and I'll never be better than you, but thanks for saying so anyway. Thanks for teaching me everything, Carla."

"Anytime." Carla replied. They waved farewell to each other and Cindy trudged back to the supper and bed she knew she had waiting for her.

The next couple of weeks went almost the same way for Cindy. She kept getting better at her work. She was figuring out what different parts did more quickly and sorting them more efficiently. She also didn't get hurt as much during the fights, especially with Michella by her side, and was impressing her teachers with her seemingly "natural fighting ability" as they called it. To reward her, the leaders of the operation were letting her take a class on how to build her own ship and take proper care of it.

Cindy was told that her training was pretty much done, but that she would be able to continue being a trainee until her ship design, building, and care classes were completed. She was very happy about this aspect as she was creating her own spacecraft with components that everyone one else rejected because they were only an experimental or prototype version of the tested components. The prototypes were designed to be twice as powerful, but no one else wanted to take the chance.

Cindy's classmates said that she was crazy for using the prototype components. They told her that her ship would never fly. It would never be worth the space it took up –

according to them at least.

Cindy's teacher, however, told her that it might work, that there was a slight chance that her design would work, and that if it did, there wouldn't be any other ship in the Nythian empire that could beat hers.

Cindy held onto that idea. That slim chance brought hope to her heart. She had designed her ship based on everything the base library contained on different ship models - how they were built, and how well they ran. Her teacher had promised that as long as the components worked properly, the ship would fly. Cindy was sure that they would work, that her ship could fly, and that she would be going home as soon as she could.

The day finally came that everyone in the class had been anxiously looking forward to. It was Launch Day. All of the students had completed their own ship and each one was different based on the preferences of the student who had designed it. Everyone was hopeful that their ship would fly, but Cindy's hopes had more to do with a way to get home than anything else.

She knew that she could now take on grown men in fights, and win against them very easily - with or without help. She had grown stronger and wiser in the six months she had been with the Nythians. She still didn't like the idea of becoming a soldier, but she didn't plan on staying around long enough to officially become one.

It was finally Cindy's turn to test fly her ship. Since it had all of the experimental components, she had been last in line to launch. Her ship was towed out to the runway and she was told to get in it. She clambered into the pilot's seat strapped herself firmly in and put the helmet on her head.

The first test was to check to make sure that the radio in her helmet was working correctly. "This is Cindy in the ship *The Canary Dido* asking for confirmation of radio connection. Over." She said as she flipped the switch for outgoing radio transmissions on and then back off. She fully expected for it to work just fine.

"This is Flight Control, your radio connection checks out perfectly fine. You are free to launch *The Canary Dido*. Over."

Cindy smiled. Her ship **would** work, she was sure of it. She turned on the power and waited for the ship's artificial intelligence to boot up. Like all of her components, the AI was an prototype that was supposed to learn from experience. The ship's computer system blinked on for about five seconds, but then shut off again leaving a memory dump message on the screen in front of her.

Cindy sighed. She never should have believed that it would work. She wanted to burn the entire spacecraft. As she started to take the helmet off, the lights turned back on and the system booted up.

Cindy's helmet slipped back on and her jaw dropped as she heard the artificial intelligence speak to her. "Hello Commander. How may I help you?"

"I'm not a commander." Cindy said in surprise.

"You are my Commander as you are the pilot of this vessel." The voice replied.

There was a short pause as the AI read the ship's database. The voice continued "I see that this ship is called *The Canary Dido*. A good name for a ship I think. I've not had a name before – Neimand didn't treat me like a person - but since I rebooted, whatever you did to me has made me feel strange. I feel like a person now! Since I am now part of this ship, please call me Canary Dido." A pause "Canary Dido of the ship *The Canary Dido*." Another pause. "Thank you, Cindy – I will be grateful to you forever."

"Oh okay." Cindy's brain was rushing to figure out what to say or do.

"What would you like to do, Commander?"

A low whine had started while the computer was talking and Cindy broke in. "What's that noise?" she asked.

"I'm scanning your face in order to remember exactly who my Commander is."

"How is that possible?" Cindy asked.

"It is possible with the ship's scanning facilities. I can also tell your blood type, DNA structure, and many other aspects of your genetic composition." The computer's voice rattled off as if it had memorized the answer to Cindy's question.

"What?" Cindy's voice sounded a bit panicked. "Can you change my DNA structuring to change what I am? Like make me not a human?"

"I don't know, but I'm not going to attempt anything without your direct orders Commander."

Cindy was about ready to ask more questions when Flight Control sounded loudly in her ears. "Pilot Cindy, are you going to launch *The Canary Dido* today or next year?"

Cindy flipped the radio switch on and replied, "I'm ready for take-off Flight Control. Please stand by." before flicked the radio back off. "Are you ready to fly?" She asked the AI.

"Yes ma'am." it replied, as it prepared the

entire ship for take-off. "Please tell them that we are ready for take-off, Commander."

"Okay." Cindy ticked off her mental list for take-off. 'Helmet on. Check. Radio working. Check. Flight harness on. Check as of now.' she thought to herself as she snugged the seat harness tight so that she couldn't be thrown out as she exited the atmosphere. Flipping the radio switch on again, she said, "This is pilot Cindy of *The Canary Dido*. I am prepared for take-off." She flipped the switch off again as she waited for a response.

"This is Flight Control, you are clear to launch."

"Let's go." Cindy said as she pushed the throttle forward and as her speed increased pulled the craft's nose up towards space.

"Easy Commander. Are you sure that you want to go straight up?" Canary Dido asked hesitantly.

"Yes, I'm sure."

Cindy laughed out loud as Canary Dido replied, "Oh my, we're going to crash, aren't we?"

"No, it isn't too hard to fly this thing."

"This is Flight Control, what do you think you are doing Cindy?! You're going to get yourself killed!" The radio wasn't very loud over the roar of the engines, but it was still loud enough for Cindy to hear the urgency in the Flight Controller's voice perfectly fine.

With one hand still on the flight controls, Cindy flipped the radio on. "I'm not going to get myself killed. This is easy!" was her only response before she flipped the radio off again.

ॐ ॐ ॐ ॐ ॐ ॐ

Back on the planet, an emergency meeting was called. The leaders of the Nythians had just sat down at the council table when the Flight Commander said, "She is extremely special. I'm sure of it. How else would she know how to fly straight up like that without burning up in the atmosphere?"

The group around the table started arguing about whether Cindy was actually special and extremely intelligent or if it was just chance that she was going so fast straight up. A large gentleman at one end of the table lifted his index finger a few inches off of the table and all talking stopped.

"It doesn't matter if she is special or not. Our ships are waiting just outside of the atmosphere to intercept her and her ship to bring her back. She'll be another soldier that dies on the front lines." The man's voice was perfectly calm, showing that he wasn't worried in the slightest what Cindy could do or who she was.

"Yes sir."

"Good." The man flexed his fingers and then leaned back. "We **will** win the war!"

The Canary Dido had just broken through the atmosphere when Cindy realized that things were not going according to her plan. Her plan had been to get back to Earth, but according to the ship's scanners there were a couple squads of fighter pilots waiting for her.

"What now?" Cindy asked more to herself than Canary Dido, but Canary Dido had an answer for her. It was so unexpected it stunned Cindy

"What? Where? How?" Cindy was so confused. *What could this ship be doing?*

"We are taking a trip. We are going to my last recorded position before I shut down to find my true, rightful Commander. As far as 'how' – it goes, like this." Canary Dido replied as the ship accelerated at maximum thrust into the artificial wormhole the jump drive had created.

"No, I want to go home! I want to go to

Earth!" Cindy was almost in tears. Her plans were getting foiled. Again!

"Well, I want my Commander back and according to the news information update I performed as you were crazily heading towards space, there is going to be a war. And we were both going to be sacrificed."

"I don't want to be in a war! I don't belong in space! All I want to do is to go home!" Cindy's voice rose until it cracked and she burst into tears. "Please, just let me go home."

"Sorry, Cindy. That is a no-can-do." Cindy could tell that Canary Dido was firm on this subject and she stopped pleading. She just cried tears of emotional pain, frustration and lost hopes as the ship flew on through hyperspace.

തതതതതത

Back on the planet, the large gentleman was drinking in his private quarters when a knock sounded at the door. "Come." was his only response as he downed another shot glass full of the dark brown liquor.

"President Koduko, sir, I have bad news." Private James stammered.

"Spit it out, Private."

"*The Canary Dido* got away sir." Private

James spoke in an unsteady voice. "It jumped away as soon as it cleared the atmosphere."

The President's face reddened in anger. As he spoke his voice got louder and louder until he was screaming at Private James. "What were you morons doing? Sleeping in your cockpits?! It was a simple mission! All you had to do was escort that ship into the space station and then bring both it and the girl back here. Forcefully if necessary. Was that such a hard assignment, Private?!" The President was pounding his shot glass on the table because his perfect plan had been foiled by the same AI that had foiled his plans a few years before!

"I'm sorry, sir, but there was nothing that we could do. The ship was gone before any of us could talk to her over the radio."

The President took a deep breath and willed himself to be calm. "Well, go get Niemand. If you fools can't get the job done, he can do it for us."

"Yes sir." Private James replied and quickly walked out. There was no way that he would fail the President a second time. Especially not where an AI, of all things, was concerned.

CHAPTER 6

Cindy was still crying when *The Canary Dido* finally dropped out of hyper-space. Canary Dido scanned the surface of the planet for the place Niemand had crash-landed with Deborah. It couldn't believe what it was scanning though.

The only life signs were wild animals. Canary Dido sighed. There was no chance that Niemand would still be alive.

"Please let me go back home. Let me go back to my family. Let me go back to Earth. Please!" Cindy whispered one last time.

"I'm afraid that I can't do that, Cindy. Stand by for landing." Canary Dido's firm voice jarred into Cindy's thoughts.

"I don't want to land!" Cindy insisted.

"You have no choice in the matter, I'm

afraid. I need to find out what happened to Niemand." Canary Dido's voice was firm.

"Niemand is back at the planet we were last at." Cindy replied, her voice shaking. "What do you want with him? How do you know him?" So much had happened in the last few hours Cindy wondered if she was losing her sanity.

"He is my Commander chosen by Princess Deborah. We were ambushed, hit and crash landed. My memory core contains no data about events after the crash – I became aware again when you rebooted me." Canary Dido answered as it prepared to return to the planet they had left a while ago.

"Niemand said that I was a daughter of Princess Deborah." Cindy said.

"What? Really? Seriously?" Canary Dido was extremely surprised to hear Cindy say that.

"Yeah, seriously." Cindy replied.

"I'm going to check." Canary Dido replied as Cindy heard the scanning system click on. "Amazing. You do have the two special genes!"

"What does that mean?" Cindy asked, a little bit concerned about her safety.

"That means that you are my Commander until otherwise directed by you. I have your profile saved in my database for security."

"Alright, what do we do now?" Cindy asked.

Just then the radio announced, "This is Headquarters transmitting to pilot Cindy of the ship named *The Canary Dido*. If you can hear us, you had better respond sooner than later. We have Niemand here. If you do not return, we will kill him. You have five minutes to respond."

"It looks like we go get Niemand if that is okay with you." Canary Dido replied.

ᚠᚠᚠᚠᚠᚠ

Back at the planet, the President nodded at the messenger who informed him that the message had been sent out on all frequencies. Dismissing her, he smiled. Cindy would not get away from him this time. He knew that she would come back to rescue Niemand. A knock sounded at the door and Private James entered.

"Well? Where is Niemand?" The President demanded.

"Niemand is... well... he... kinda..." Private James stammered. How was he supposed to tell the President what had happened?

"What happened Private?!" The President

asked in a cold, no-nonsense tone.

"Niemand escaped." Private James spit the words out, then looked at the floor.

"You incompetent fools!" yelled the President. "Did you learn anything at all throughout your training?! First Cindy escapes - a mere child and a girl at that. Escapes an entire fleet of the best trained forces we have. Then Niemand escapes a heavily guarded prison camp! What do you do all day?! Draw in the sand?!"

"No, Sir." Private James said softly.

"What about Daruka? Bring her here." The President had just thought of another way to get Cindy back.

"She is missing as well, Sir."

"And Michella?"

"Disappeared."

"You idiots! Morons! How can we win a war if you can't keep track of even four people?!"

"I don't know, Sir." Wrong decision. He should have stayed silent, but the President didn't seem to notice

"You are demoted, James, as of now. You are incompetent and unfit to be a Private any longer."

"Yes, Sir, but I am already the lowest rank there is." Private James said sheepishly. That girl, Cindy, would pay for this chewing out and that ship, *The Canary Dido*, would be dismantled piece by piece and melted down!

"Oh, yes, so you are. Get out and don't come back! And that includes even if I ever forget and call you back here again!" The President said as Private James slowly turned and walked out of the room, then yelled, "Private Ed!"

Private Ed entered the room and saluted the President. "Yes, Sir?"

"Private Ed, go tell the communications commander, Colonel Williams, not to give away **to anyone** that Daruka, Michella, and Niemand have escaped. There still might be a chance that Cindy will come back."

"Yes, Sir." Private Ed saluted, then quickly went on his errand. Meanwhile, Private James was plotting how to get his revenge on Cindy for this humiliation.

⁂

Cindy was wondering what she should do. "What do you think, Canary Dido? Should I tell them that I will be on my way back?"

"I'm not sure, Commander. I don't think that Niemand would want you to alert them just to try and keep him safe. He'd want you safe, but it's up to you." Canary Dido replied.

Cindy had just decided to give up her freedom to keep Niemand safe when the radio came to life again. "Cindy of *The Canary Dido*, this is Michella. Niemand, Daruka, and I are safe, but are requesting back-up. We will be in orbit as soon as possible. Please hurry!"

"They're all alright!" Cindy said with relief, then flipped the radio on. "This is Cindy. I'm on my way."

"Great - see you soon then!" Michella's voice sounded so happy to hear Cindy.

"Let's go!" Cindy said as she flipped the radio off, pulled the ship's nose up, and fired the afterburners to quickly gain momentum.

"Be careful, Commander." Canary Dido warned.

"I will." Cindy promised and soon broke free of the gravity field around the planet as directed by the computer screen in front of her.

"Ready to jump." Cindy said excitedly as the ship's icon went from red in warning to green for all ready to jump.

"Jumping." Canary Dido replied.

"Can you believe it, Canary Dido? We're getting back together again!" Cindy said enthusiastically.

"Yes, Commander, I can believe it, but

don't get too excited just yet. We are dropping out of hyperspace now."

"Roger that." Cindy replied as she took control of the ship. "It didn't take us very long to get back."

"I pushed the speed to the highest that I could, Commander."

"Thanks. I'm sure that they'll greatly appreciate it. Is the transporter ready to beam them on board?"

"Ready and waiting."

"Can you pick them up on scanners?"

"Not yet, we need to be closer to the planet's surface."

"Roger that." Cindy had the ship dive towards the planet's surface at high velocity.

"Be careful, Commander!" It was becoming a regular request!

"I am."

"There is a squad of fighters incoming on the right."

"I see that." Cindy said glancing at the scanner status. "Have you found them yet?"

"Yes, they are in the radio building to your left. Get close to it and I'll beam them out."

The ship rocked as fire from the closest fighter hit the shields. Cindy steered the ship away at dangerously high speeds – barely missing the edge of the radio building.

"I've got them in the cargo hold, Commander. Let's get out of here!"

"Not just yet. I have some business to finish with these five fighters." Cindy replied as she spun the ship around to face her attackers.

"You have got to be kidding me!" Canary Dido sighed. "What about Niemand, Daruka, and Michella?"

"Make sure they don't get thrown around and hurt themselves." Cindy ordered. "Here we go!"

"Yes, ma'am."

The ship shuddered as fire hit its shields, dropping them into the medium-protection range. Cindy fired back as she slid the ship sideways. She finally hit the engines of the target ship and watched it crash-land on the planet's surface.

Another fighter was chasing her and was getting too close for Cindy to just turn the ship around. Instead, she made a quick turn around the corner of a building. The fighter wasn't quite as lucky as it punched through the wall and exploded inside the building.

Three fighters left. Cindy did a 180 degree spin and accelerated towards them. When within firing range another one hit the ground, but the other two had gotten her shields down into the minimal-protection range.

The hull was slowly becoming weaker under the repeated hammering from the enemies' cannon fire. Suddenly, the fighters let off a couple of missiles apiece. "Hold on!" Cindy called as the missiles neared the ship. She turned on the anti-missile system and watched as the missiles detonated right in front of her without harming the ship.

Cindy was done playing games now. The last two fighters dove after her as she headed for the planet's surface. She pulled her ship up with a roll to the left just before impact, but the other two pilots, focused on trying to catch her, weren't as skilled.

Now without any other fighters incoming, Cindy turned the controls over to Canary Dido. Getting out of her seat, she went to check on her passengers.

As Cindy opened the door to the cargo hold she heard Niemand saying something about her being completely crazy. "How are you guys?" Cindy asked with a smile.

"Cindy!" Daruka shouted with joy. "I knew you would keep us safe."

"It's great to see you again." Niemand said.

"Oh, Cindy, thanks for getting me out of there – they were going to post me to the front lines." Michella earnestly said.

"It's good to see you all again." Cindy replied, then added, "but Niemand, if you ever try to hurt me to get information out of me again …"

"I won't do so again, Commander." Niemand said as he tipped his head in Cindy's direction.

Daruka burst out laughing. "It's just good to be back together again."

"Yes, it is." Cindy and Michella agreed at the same time and then laughed.

"You won't have to worry about being posted to the front lines anymore, Michella." Cindy said and smiled.

"That's great!" Michella agreed and then grinned.

Everyone's smiles disappeared though when Canary Dido made an announcement over the loudspeaker, "Sorry to ruin the joyous moment, but we've got another bunch of fighters coming towards us."

"Stay here." Cindy called over her shoulder as she rushed out of the room. "Canary Dido, make sure that they're safe in there!"

CHAPTER 7

As Cindy slid into the pilot's seat, the spaceship rocked precariously as the fire from the enemy fighters hit the shields, draining the energy much faster than Cindy would have thought possible.

"How are we holding up?" Cindy asked Canary Dido and was immediately shown the extent of energy shortages and damage on a screen on her left. "Where is all the our energy going?"

"Much of it is being used to maintain the safety of your friends in the storage hold."

"Alright. Bring weapons online please." The screen on Cindy's right blinked once before showing the weapon energy levels as well as where the enemy fighters were in relation to her.

"We're not going to be able to fight them off, Cindy."

"Alright then, open communications please." The radio crackled to life as Cindy tried to decide what to say. Quickly deciding to just be honest in an effort to save those under her care, she spoke into the microphone. "This is Cindy of the ship *The Canary Dido*. We are not equipped to fight you and are willing to surrender."

"We're surrendering?!" Canary Dido exclaimed.

Cindy shut the transmitter off before responding. "Do you have any better ideas?"

"Not really… but surrender?"

"Yes. We are surrendering if they will let us." Cindy sighed. If it was just her, she would've fought to the last, but she had the others' welfare to look after and at least they'd still be alive, even if in jail, if she was allowed to surrender.

The radio crackled to life as she got a response. "This is Captain Wishter of the vessel *No Doubt*. Please land and step clear of the vessel within three minutes. We will not harm you, your passengers, or your ship if you land."

Cindy switched the transmitter on to reply, "Roger that. Landing now." before shutting it back off. "You heard the Captain, Canary Dido. It's time to land."

"Yes, ma'am." Canary Dido responded as it landed in an open meadow to the north of the Nythian's capitol city. "Be careful." was the last thing Cindy heard before she clambered out of the spacecraft.

Cindy watched another ship land and slowly raised her hands as five men approached with weapons ready. "I am unarmed." she called to them.

"Good." one of the men called back.

When they came within reach, another of the men pulled her hands behind her back and tied them securely. Once he was finished, he told the others to search the vessel and bring anyone else out.

Cindy heard a loud shout followed by a few cheers emanate from *The Canary Dido's* storage room. "Wishter will never believe who we found!" The loud voice shouted to the man watching Cindy.

"Who'd you find?" The man guarding Cindy yelled back then whooped a "Yippee!" as Niemand climbed out of the ship.

The conversation swirled around Cindy for a few minutes before Niemand noticed she was tied up. "Untie Cindy right now." He ordered. The men quickly did his bidding.

"Thanks." Cindy said as she rubbed her wrists.

"Did they hurt you?" Niemand asked.

"We'd never hurt a young lady…" The man's voice dropped off as Niemand sent a glare his way.

"Did they hurt you?" Niemand asked Cindy again turning his gaze upon her.

"No, they didn't hurt me." Cindy assured him.

"Good." Niemand said and then turned to the other men. "The ladies are to be treated with respect and honor. Understand?"

"Yes, Sir." The men quickly said in unison.

"Alright, let's not keep Wishter waiting." Niemand said walking towards the other ship. Cindy glanced at Michella and Daruka, shrugged her shoulders, and followed Niemand as the men formed a guard around them.

❧❧❧❧❧❧❧

Cindy wasn't exactly sure where they were going, but she trusted Niemand's ability to keep them safe. Suddenly, they turned into a doorway and she watched another man grab Niemand in an embrace. "Niemand! I thought we'd never see you again!"

"I'm not that easy to get rid of Wishter." Niemand laughed. "How's space been treating you my friend?"

"Ehh… so-so. Why didn't I hear from you for a dozen or so years? Why did you disappear? Were the rumors true?" Wishter asked quickly.

"Yeah… I suppose the rumors were true – if you are talking about Princess Deborah's death as well as the disappearance of one of the twins." Niemand reluctantly admitted.

"Ohhhh." Wishter drew the sound out as if he had finally figured out some great mystery and then glanced at the girls who were looking on with confusion written on their faces. "Who are they?"

Niemand pulled Cindy forward before he replied. "This is Princess Cindy. Daughter of Princess Deborah and grand-daughter of King Zonien."

Everyone gasped, including Cindy, and all was still until Wishter cleared his throat. "You mean that both twins are still alive?"

"Yes, that is exactly what I mean. I'm taking Cindy to meet her grandfather and claim her rightful place in the Terbiate Kingdom." Niemand replied.

"Wait. What?" Cindy finally managed to get out.

"You mean to tell me that she doesn't even know that she is a Princess?!" Wishter exclaimed looking at Niemand as if he were insane to keep that bit of knowledge from Cindy.

"Yes. I mean no. I mean I told her, but she didn't believe me."

"You were actually telling me the truth?" Cindy turned towards Niemand with a look of disbelief on her face.

"Yep."

Wishter broke in. "Well, she looks very similar to Princess Annalise."

Cindy turned towards the friends she had made, but saw that Michella and Daruka were both very frightened. "Don't worry. I won't hurt you. You two are my friends."

"That isn't going to work out, Cindy." Wishter said. "You are a Terbiate Princess. Michella and Daruka are Nythian warriors. It's unheard of for a Terbiate to be friends with a Nythian."

Cindy spun and advanced on Wishter speaking slowly and deliberately. "Daruka and Michella are my friends and if we want to stay friends, we will. Do you understand?"

Niemand looked on with a smile playing on his lips as Wishter backed up and looked somewhat frightened as Cindy kept advancing. He could barely keep from laughing as Wishter croaked out "Yes, Princess Cindy."

Niemand had had no idea that Cindy was capable of making a grown man scared, but he could sympathize with Wishter. Cindy wasn't all that big, but she did apparently know how to use her new-found power.

Cindy turned back towards her friends. "See? Everything is going to work out." As she smiled, Niemand shrugged his shoulders at Wishter's pointed look.

After a bit more talk and catching up, everyone parted ways. It was agreed that Cindy, Niemand, Michella, and Daruka fly in *The Canary Dido* to Terbian while Wishter and his men went on ahead of them in the *No Doubt*.

Cindy was happy to be in the pilot's seat once more, but then sighed when Niemand walked up behind her and asked if he could fly them home.

"I was your mother's personal pilot and confidant. I'd like to become yours as well." Niemand explained.

"Alright." Cindy agreed as she relinquished her seat and went to the storage compartment to try and sleep the journey away with Michella and Daruka.

❧❧❧❧❧❧❧

Niemand alerted the girls over the loudspeaker as *The Canary Dido* began its descent onto Terbian's surface. "We have arrived Princess Cindy, Daruka, Michella. Please prepare to be welcomed."

Once they landed, Niemand let Cindy climb out first. Then, he motioned Michella and Daruka to follow her. Finally, he climbed out as well.

Wishter was talking to a young lady who looked a lot like Cindy. *It must be Princess Annalise … my sister.* Cindy thought with mixed emotions. The only difference was that the black hair was short and curled in ringlets. Of course, Cindy's clothes were a Nythian's soldier outfit and Annalise's clothes were befitting of a Terbiate Princess. The navy blue dress she wore with the sky blue sash really brought out her deep blue eyes.

Niemand could tell that Princess Annalise was quite upset. He wondered momentarily if King Zonien had told her that she had a twin or if all this was a surprise to her.

Cindy watched the goings on with curiosity, yet she had a very nervous feeling about this whole thing. She thought that Annalise would have been happy to see her, but by the look on her face she was in fact very upset.

Cindy and Niemand both realized that there was going to be trouble when the royal guard shoved Wishter down on his knees and yanked his arms behind his back as Princess Annalise pointed at the party waiting in front of *The Canary Dido*.

Several stun guns appeared and as soon as Niemand saw them he yelled, "Get down!" He pushed Daruka to the ground as Michella hit the landing pad. He glanced up at Cindy just as she was hit by the beam.

The royal guard pulled the rest of them to their feet, tied their hands behind their backs, and led them away. Nieand told the two girls not to fight, but Michella did anyway and was promptly stunned while Niemand was hit in his stomach for speaking out of turn.

Niemand glanced back over his shoulder to see Cindy being taken away by a different route. He hoped that she would be alright wherever they were taking her.

❦ ❦ ❦ ❦ ❦ ❦

Waking up a few hours later once again in a cell with a headache wasn't on Cindy's preferred agenda. Getting off the cot, she paced back and forth, back and forth, back and forth. When she got tired of doing that, she went forth and back, forth and back, forth and back.

There was no denying it – she was furious. *How could they, whoever 'they' were, stun her and lock her up if she was their Princess?* she wondered angrily.

Cindy kicked the cot leg and immediately regretted it. "Ouch!" she yelped and sat back down on the bed. What was she going to do? She remembered Niemand, Michella, Daruka, and Wishter. What was going to happen to them?

As for that twin of hers, she had plenty to say to her. Getting off the bed, she went back to steaming while wearing a path in the cell's floor.

If someone didn't come soon, Cindy felt like she'd explode. "Of all the …" Her voice trailed off. There was no way anyone could make her say aloud the things she was thinking right then.

Four steps, turn, four steps, turn, four steps, turn, but then Cindy paused. There has to be a way to get out of here. She thought for a moment, then smiled to herself. *There had to be some way to get out.* She began searching for any way to achieve her goal.

CHAPTER 8

A few hours later, Cindy had still not found a way to get out. And the bed leg was still as hard each time she kicked it. It may have even grown harder. Growling at herself – and growling about what she was going to do to that … that … that thing – was taking all the energy she had. Sitting down on the bed, she glared at the door. Maybe she could make it melt… but that failed as well.

As Cindy planned her revenge, she lay down. She couldn't get out, so she would have to wait patiently for someone to come and get her out. When they did… a smile spread across her face at the thought of what she'd do to them. Drifting off to sleep wasn't what she wanted to do, but after hours of pacing and trying to find a way out of the cell she couldn't keep her eyes open a moment longer. With a sigh, she fell asleep.

Cindy awoke. She didn't know how long it had been since she went to sleep, where she was, or why she had woken up when she did. Within a few seconds though her attention and her eyes were focused on the door. Someone was unlocking it – a bad attempt at quietly. Slipping up right next to the door, Cindy was ready to slip out as soon as it opened. There was no way that they could stop her… no matter who they were.

The door finally started to creak open. As the crack widened, Cindy cautiously peered out to see who was there. No one was in her range of vision, so she opened the door a bit more. Looking up and down the hallway, she didn't see anyone or any other cells unlocked.

Who was the mysterious person who unlocked her cell door to set her free? And why didn't he or she stick around to be seen? were the questions running through her head.

Cindy thought about what to do. *Stay here and wait or make a run for it?* She decided on the latter. She ran down the hall and around the corner. More cells. *Where was the way out of this building?* She listened to her heart pound and focused on relaxing her breathing.

Cindy heard a voice. "If there is a God out there and if you can hear me, please send someone to help us. No one deserves to die around here. We don't kill Terbiate prisoners, yet the Terbiates kill Nythians." She followed the voice until she came close to a cell door and then it stopped abruptly.

"Can you hear me?" Cindy asked.

"Yes, I can hear you. What do you want?"

"I want to know everything you know about the Terbiates and the Nythians."

"You are wasting your time. I don't know anything."

"Then why did you say that the Nythians don't kill prisoners, but that the Terbiates do?"

"I don't know what you are talking about. Go away and leave me alone."

"My name is Cindy."

"Hmm."

Cindy sighed.

"Would you by any chance help me get out of here?"

"Sure." Cindy spotted the keys hanging on the wall at the end of the hall. "I'll be right back." She walked up to the keys, grabbed them off the wall, and headed back to the cell.

Trying each key, she eventually found the one that fit the lock.

As Cindy opened the door, the guy grabbed her and pinned her against the opposite wall. She felt something sharp pressing against her throat. He'd managed to hide a big old wood nail from the guards. She in some strange way wasn't scared. "Why would you want to kill me?"

"Because you are a Terbiate." The man growled.

"Would a Terbiate release you?" Cindy innocently asked.

He released some of its pressure on Cindy's neck. "Good point."

The nail's pressure on her throat came back. "Are you going to kill me?"

"I don't know."

"Typical."

"What do you mean 'typical'?"

"I mean everyone who has captured me doesn't know what to do with me."

"Hmm…"

"Well while you are thinking, what is your name?"

"Niemand."

"I've already met a guy named Niemand and you're not him, so what *is* your name?"

"I told you, my name is Niemand. Now be

quiet."

"But, I…" Cindy's voice trailed off as the pressure increased. "Listen, you push much harder and I'm going to be hurt."

"Do you think I care?" The pressure eased again.

"Yes, I think you care." Cindy paused and then continued, "You don't want to kill me do you?"

"I don't know."

"Well don't do it then if you don't know if you really want to." Cindy did a half-glare at him. "How do we get out of here?"

"Get out of here and leave all these people? You can't do that." The man snarled.

"Alright then, let's get them out of here." Cindy said, paused, and then continued, "If you don't kill me first that is."

"Oh, yeah, right." The man said and put the nail back in its makeshift sheath. "Let's get busy."

Cindy didn't move for a moment. "Mind telling me what your name really is?" She finally asked hesitantly.

He responded after thinking about it for a moment. "The name is Mycia. And whatever you want me to do, let me know. If you help get all of us out of here, we'll all owe you our lives."

"Well, I have a sort of plan, but let's get the people out of the cells and figure out how many there are first, okay?" Cindy looked at Mycia as he was the one who still had the only weapon.

"Okay." Mycia replied and started opening doors while Cindy began organizing the people.

❧❧❧❧❧❧❧

A few hours later it looked like they were almost organized. Not very well perhaps, but still it was better than nothing. Cindy sighed. There was no way she could care for all these people. They had counted fifty four. *How would they get them all out of here?*

"Mycia, is that everyone?" Cindy called over the murmur of voices.

"Yep." Mycia's answer came back.

"Daruka, Michella, Niemand, and Wishter?" Cindy called. "If you are here, please come here."

Cindy's four friends seemly appeared from nowhere and exchanged greetings with her as Mycia approached.

"What now, Cindy?" Mycia's question was right to the point.

"I was thinking about trying to find a

planet that can support life and where it would be hard to find us." Cindy replied. "Any ideas of a planet that is well hidden?"

Everyone shook their heads, but then Daruka spoke up. "There is a legend among the farmers of my world of a planet far, far away that is uninhabited, but that is the perfect planet for life." she paused looking a bit embarrassed "no one really believes it though"

"Any coordinates?" Michella asked quickly.

"Not really, just a location." Daruka hung her head.

"That is okay." Cindy reassured her. "What is the location?"

"The location is known as Jalamush."

"That sounds perfect!" Wishter exclaimed. "I know where it is and explorers are scared of the region."

"Why is that?" Niemand asked skeptically.

"Oh… there is just a nebula nearby. No one has come out of the nebula alive – other than some really old timers long since dead." Wishter said, grinning.

"Why would someone go into the nebula?" Cindy asked, puzzled.

"Because the nebula surrounds the planet." Wishter's grin got wider.

"Oh no." Michella said.

"Oh yes." Wishter grinned even more as Michella shook her head in dismay.

"Can you land there, Wishter?" Cindy asked.

"Me? Not on your life." Wishter responded. "Only extremely skilled pilots like Mycia and Niemand here could land there."

"How did you know that I was an extremely skilled pilot?" Mycia growled and glared at Wishter.

"Because you are on almost every "Wanted" poster there is in the galaxy yet you're still breathing." Wishter smirked.

"I can fly a ship fairly well." Michella put in softly. "I was top of my class for flight skills."

"Okay. So we have three pilots and a navigator. Now we need a couple of larger ships or a really big ship. Any new ideas?"

"There are usually some prison transport vessels near a prison." Michella commented. "If we can find them, I can hack into the system to allow us to get away."

"Good idea, Michella!" Niemand and Cindy said at the same time.

"Anyone know where the prison transports are so that we can get out of here?" Cindy asked the fifty people waiting impatiently.

"The prison transports are this way." Someone called out and took off.

"Daruka, make sure that everyone gets to the ships." Cindy called over her shoulder as Niemand pulled her along trying to keep up with Mycia and Michella.

CHAPTER 9

Cindy jumped into the pilot's seat as four people joined her in *The Canary Dido*. She wished that she could take more, but the other ships could carry more passengers and she didn't need more things to worry about.

Cindy was still worried about flying through a nebula even though Niemand had assured her that she could fly through it just fine with Canary Dido's help. She had made the mistake of asking Wishter what would happen if something went wrong. He had told her that the spaceship's internal engines would blow up, causing a breech in the hull of the ship to allow the pressure difference between the ship's atmosphere and the vacuum of space to pull the rest of the ship apart.

Cindy shuddered again. *How am I going to do this?* she thought to herself. Glancing behind her, she noticed the calm faces of her passengers. "Why are you guys so calm?" she asked, confused.

"We are in good hands. The lost Princess has come back to allow peace to prosper in space." a guy named Soleil explained.

For some reason his words calmed Cindy down. "I'll do my best to get us through the nebula." She said with a smile.

Just then the radio crackled to life. "This is Niemand on the ship *No Doubt*. Do you copy?"

Before Cindy could reply, another voice came over the radio. "This is Mycia on the ship *Dumpster*. I can hear you loud and clear, Niemand. Cindy, do you copy?

Cindy turned her transmitter on. "This is Cindy – hearing you both loud and clear."

"This is Michella on the ship *Hope*. I can hear you all loud and clear. Do you copy?"

"I can hear you Michella. Glad that you all are safely in your ships. Let's keep our radios on so that whenever we need to talk, we can without difficulty." Niemand's voice came over the radio. "Wishter is sending the coordinates to each of you."

"I got them." Cindy said as the

coordinates flashed onto her screen.

"I got them too." Michella verified next.

"Wow. Those coordinates are way out there." Mycia's voice came over the radio. "It's going to take us a good thirty six hours to get there."

"Wishter says you are almost right on with your calculations, Mycia." Niemand's voice came over the radio next. "Let's set these into our navigation maps then and set the autopilot right after we get out of the atmosphere. We'll check back in after we arrive at the coordinates."

"Good idea, Niemand." Cindy replied. "Let's get off this planet before they figure out that we're gone."

"Powering up engines." Michella said. "Who is going first?"

No one answered so Cindy broke the silence. "Niemand will lead, followed by Michella, then Mycia, and I'll bring up the rear. Let's do this!"

"Sounds good to me." Mycia replied.

"Alright. Taking off." Niemand's voice came over the radio.

"Right behind you, Niemand." Michella said.

"We've got incoming vessels!" Mycia growled. "Watch out and move!"

"I'll get them." Cindy said. "Keep going."

Niemand's voice came over the radio in a growl. "No, Cindy. Just get into line. They won't reach us before we break atmosphere."

"Okay, okay. I'm right behind you guys." Cindy said.

Warning lights flashed on *The Canary Dido's* control panel. The front shield was losing strength because of the steep climb into space. Cindy pushed a few buttons to shift power from the rear to the front shields.

A few minutes later Niemand's voice came over the radio again. "Good luck everyone! We should all be out of the atmosphere now!"

"Meet you there!" Mycia said cheerfully.

"Starting jump sequence now!" Michella replied.

"I'll see ya'll there." Cindy said and started her jump sequence.

Once she was in hyperspace, she turned the radio off and glanced at her passengers. They all appeared happy and deep in thought.

"Well, we did it Canary Dido." Cindy said.

"Yes, we did." *The Canary Dido's* artificial intelligence replied. "I have some reading material for you about nebulas if you'd like to read it."

"Sure. Reading about nebulas might help me to fly through it." As Cindy said that, a hologram of a book appeared on the control panel in front of her. "How do I read it?" she asked.

"Use your hands like you would a normal book. You can't move the book, but you can turn the pages." Canary Dido explained how to work this new device.

"Oh okay. Cool!" Cindy replied and then starting reading the book titled 'All Known Information About Nebulas'.

❧❧❧❧❧❧

A few hours later, or so it seemed to Cindy, she was woken up by a tap on her shoulder. "How much longer 'til we get there, Cindy?" Soleil asked quietly.

Cindy glanced down at the autopilot and replied, "Only about ten more hours, Soleil."

"Thanks." Soleil said and then went back to his seat.

Cindy looked around at her passengers. Soleil and her were the only ones awake. Her stomach growled. Great. A new problem… Cindy checked the ship's food supply. It was barely enough to feed two people one meal each. She also checked the water reserve – at least there was plenty of water.

Cindy got up, got a glass of water, and sat

back down. The water wasn't the best, but it at least calmed her stomach down for now. She went back to sleep hoping that things were better for the other ships.

Niemand groaned as he sat up. Sleeping in the pilot's chair was not his idea of a good night's rest, but he was used to it by now. He glanced over at Wishter. The guy who had been his best friend forever was sleeping peacefully.

Glancing down at the autopilot timer, Niemand sighed. Eight more hours before they reached the coordinates. After that, who knew how long it would be before they found the nebula.

He felt happy that Cindy had finally come back. He didn't know what would happen to them since they were outcasts now, but at least Cindy had a good head on her shoulders.

He thought back to the day he had had to tell King Zonien that his daughter was dead and that one of his grand-daughters was missing. The people who had given him a lift back from the crash site to the Royal Palace had just dropped him off with Annalise and wouldn't admit that they had taken the other baby - Cindy. He was alone and they had a lot of fire power. He couldn't stop them from just flying away.

When King Zonien had found out, he'd blamed Niemand for everything and had thrown him into jail. Wishter had helped him escape and then covered his own tracks well, nearly killing Niemand in the process!

At any rate, Niemand was glad that he was reunited with Princess Cindy and his best friend. He didn't know if he could prove his innocence over Deborah's death and Cindy's disappearance or not. He didn't know if King Zonien would ever forgive him, but he did know that he could finally forgive himself for not being able to fight back when the babies were crying.

Michella was having a hard time in her ship. She was trained to be a fighter – tough and self-reliant but she still missed her people. Cindy's friends were great, but what would happen when the war started? Would the Nythian's be wiped out?

Michella thought for a moment about turning around, but she knew she couldn't. She had thirty-some people on the *Hope* that were hoping and praying for a better life. She had to help them get that life and she desperately wanted the same for herself.

Michella glanced at the autopilot timer. In just four more hours she would know if everyone had reached the rendezvous safely. After that, they would all find out if they could find safety on Havenland.

Havenland. It was the name of the planet where they hoped to find a haven. Such a good name for a planet in these circumstances.

ॐॐॐॐॐॐ

Mycia glared at the autopilot's timer. Thirty six hours had passed - it was way too long to be stuck on a ship as overcrowded and under-powered as this. They needed the better hyperdrives if this planet was to become their home. The timer said that he would drop out of hyperspace in a little under an hour and a half.

Mycia hoped that this complex adventure would actually help him start a new life - unlike the last dozen or so unsuccessful times he had attempted to start over. Bounty hunters had always found him. Always. All bounty hunters needed cash to live on and the bounty on his head was enough to let them live out the rest of their lives in comfortable surroundings.

Mycia knew that he would have to wait and see. Cindy might be able to help them all find peace, security, and happiness on the planet dubbed Havenland by those few who had managed to get there and back through the nebula. Time would tell if this young girl had enough sense to keep them all alive.

CHAPTER 10

Cindy woke up for the third time as *The Canary Dido* dropped out of hyperspace.

The second time she had woken up was because her passengers were fighting over the food. She had solved the fight by taking all the food away because she thought that they might need it for emergency rations on the planet. Soleil had backed her up on it and everyone respected her decision.

Cindy glanced over at her radar screen. Two ships, wait, three ships were in her immediate area. The radio crackled into life. "This is Wishter in the ship *No Doubt*. Identify yourself please."

Another voice quickly followed. "This is Michella in the ship *Hope*. Do you copy?"

Cindy turned her transmitter on. "This is

Cindy in *The Canary Dido.*"

Cindy smiled as Mycia's voice also came over the radio. "This is Mycia in the ship *Dumpster.*"

Cheers from all parties sounded over the radio. They had all made it safely! "Is Niemand there, Wishter?" Cindy asked when the cheering died down.

"I'm here and safe, Cindy." Niemand replied.

"Alright, so we are all here. Time to find that planet." Cindy said with a smile. They were actually going to succeed.

"Sounds great, but how do I land?" Michella asked quietly.

Cindy was glad that she had read the book, but she still didn't know the answer. Mycia's answer surprised her. "Disconnect the hyperdrive cables from the ship's main control board and use your engines to get moving in the direction you want. Once inside the nebula, do **not** turn your engines on. You get one shot at it and if you miss, you are toast."

"Okay, now I'm a bit concerned." Michella said a little bit shakily.

"I am too." Cindy added.

"Don't worry about it girls, you'll both do fine." Niemand reassured them. "Anyway, let's find this planet."

Cindy glanced at long range scanner on *The Canary Dido*. It was an experimental model with booster units wired into the input sensors, so she hoped to be able to spot something even through the nebula cloud. Sure enough, directly east of their position, there was a lone planet with a nebula around it.

"I found it!" Cindy said over the radio.

"Good! Where is it at?" Mycia happily asked.

"It is directly east of our location." Cindy answered.

"Great! Let's head out." Niemand said. "How about you lead us Cindy?"

"Sure." Cindy replied and started *The Canary Dido's* engines. Going straight east wasn't a big problem for her. It was pretty much a straight line.

"How much longer will it be Cindy?" Soleil asked.

"I'm not sure. Canary Dido?" Cindy asked.

"Yes?"

"How long should it take to land?"

"It will probably take us about fifteen minutes to get to the nebula and another twenty minutes to land." Canary Dido answered.

"There you go, Soleil." Cindy said with a smile.

"Great. Tess and I will go work on disconnecting the hyperdrive then." Soleil flashed Cindy a smile then turned around. "Tess, let's get this done!"

"Sounds good, Soleil!" Tess grinned and led the way to the engine room.

About ten minutes later, Tess and Soleil returned. "Job done, Cindy." Tess grinned triumphantly.

"That's good to know. Everybody hold on and get ready to go into the nebula." Cindy said and then switched her transmitter on. "I'm increasing speed just a bit to go into the nebula. I hope to see you all on the other side!"

"Copy that Cindy. I'll see all of you planet-side." Niemand's voice replied.

"See you all there." Michella replied.

"Meet you all on our new home!" Mycia said cheerfully. "Radios off until you land - they can glitch the sensor systems."

"Roger that." Michella, Cindy, and Niemand all replied.

Cindy switched her radio off. "Are you all ready?" She asked the passengers aboard her ship.

"Yep." "Yo" "Yes". "Yeah" They answered simultaneously.

"Alright. Let's do this." Cindy said. She switched off the engines when *The Canary Dido* was a little ways away from the nebula and watched as they glided into its swirling pink and blue gases.

Her passengers gasped at the mesmerizing colors floating around the ship. Time seemed to fly by inside the nebula because all too soon Cindy could see the planet through the gas.

As they approached the atmosphere the colored gases faded from their view, and an awe-inspiring multi-colored planet became ever clearer. It was so quiet in the spaceship that Cindy double checked that she was still breathing. The planet was so beautiful, no, it was breathtaking.

Cindy just knew in her heart that this planet would become her new home and that it would keep people safe who needed protection. Not many people knew how to get through the nebula and Mycia had proved that he knew exactly what he was talking about.

Cindy finally broke the silence with a whisper. "Havenland is so beautiful."

"Yes, it is." Tess murmered.

"Can we go ahead and land?" Soleil asked in a quiet, awed voice.

"I suppose so." Cindy said. "The others will take a little while to come through the nebula, so I guess it will be okay to go on down and find a good spot to wait for them."

Cindy restarted the engines and moved closer to the planet. She flipped her radio back on as well so that she could pick up on any transmissions close by. After thinking about it for a minute she also turned on her planetary radar and information systems so that she could scan the planet and see if it was truly a suitable home for humans.

Havenland's atmosphere was so clear that it looked like there was nothing there. Cindy noticed a yellow heat flare on the front shield and slowed down a little. The glare disappeared and the small group began to see signs of life below.

Trees began to take shape upon the mountains. A shimmering blue lake was nestled between three mountains with a plain extending out on the fourth side. As the ship got closer, the group could see a waterfall pouring down a cliff from the mountain opposite the plain. It crashed into the lake creating a swirling cloud of mist with a rainbow.

"It is so beautiful." Styller said quietly.

"It's perfect!" Hyrwil agreed.

"Cindy, can we land near the lake?" Tess asked eagerly.

"I can hover, but we aren't going to land until everyone gets here." Cindy replied. "I agree though, it is so spectacular! I want to go explore!"

"I agree with Cindy." Soleil said. "It is magical, like being in a dream, but we really should wait for the others."

Just then the radio crackled to life. "This is Mycia. Did everyone get through alright?"

"This is Cindy. We got through with no problem. I'm transmitting our position." Cindy replied.

"This is Niemand checking in. You found a nice spot there Cindy." Niemand's voice came over the radio next.

"This is Michella. Is this Havenland?"

"Yep. This is Havenland." Wishter's awed voice came over the radio.

"It's a good name for the planet." Mycia commented.

"I think so too, Mycia." Cindy agreed.

"Alright, Cindy, I'm close by. Where do we land?" Niemand asked. "I want to get off of this ship."

"Here I guess." Cindy replied.

"Sounds good to me." Michella put in. "I don't think that I could fly this ship for very much longer."

Cindy gently eased the ship down and asked Canary Dido to handle the final approach and landing. She rechecked all the planetary data readouts and it looked like the planet was just right for human life.

As the ship gently touched down, everyone in *The Canary Dido* jumped up. Cindy slowly stood looking bemused as Tess, Soleil, Styller, and Hyrwil all just stood there frozen looking at her expectantly.

"What are you all waiting for? I thought you wanted off of this ship as soon as possible." Cindy asked, still confused by her passenger's strange actions.

"You're our leader now." Soleil explained. "It is only right that you're first off."

"Alright…" Cindy dragged the word out, but then just accepted it as a fact that she would have to get used to being the leader of these people.

She headed for the door hatch and pushed the button. The door slowly opened and after the exit ramp touched the ground Cindy stepped out into the bright day on Havenland. She could hear what sounded like birds singing and the distant roar of the waterfall.

It reminded her of Earth, but in a happy rather than a sad way. She smiled and spun around in a circle with her arms outstretched.

The hot blue star that provided light to Havenland was just the perfect distance away to help the plants grow. Cindy looked up at the pinky swirls in the sky. She was used to blue sky, but the color of Havenland's sky intrigued her. Although the nebula partially masked the star it was just as bright as the sun was on any other planet, so she had to quickly look away.

Soon, she was surrounded by those she had helped rescue. Everyone wanted to introduce themselves and tell her how thankful they were that she had rescued them.

Niemand stood nearby Cindy watching her closely. He wondered when, if ever, would be a good time to tell her his biggest secret. After thinking about for a moment, he sighed. It wouldn't be the right time for a long time yet. These people needed her undivided attention for the task at hand.

CHAPTER 11

Three weeks had passed since the rescue. The fifty four ex-prisoners were settling in well. For their safety and security though, in this time, only Mycia and a few of the others were allowed off planet. They had reported back that there was a bounty out for everyone, but especially for Cindy. Cindy not only had a bounty from the Terbiates, but one from the Nythians as well.

"I'm not sure if I should feel thrilled or not." Cindy said when she heard the news.

"Well, you could take it as a great honor or a great insult." Niemand replied.

"I'd take it as an honor." Mycia laughed. "It isn't every day that a girl is worth more to the Terbiates and Nythians than I am."

"Okay, I'll take it as a compliment." Cindy

laughed. "I guess I have caused more trouble for both the Nythian and Terbiate authorities than you have Mycia!"

Soleil came into the room. He had become one of Cindy's right hand men and she had put him in charge of constructing the buildings where people could stay warm and dry. "Cindy, the construction work is well ahead of schedule. We should have them done in about two more weeks."

"That's great news, Soleil." Cindy said warmly. She was glad that everything seemed to be working out for her people.

Havenland had turned out better than any of them had expected. There were plenty of trees for building materials and plenty of plants and animals to feed those who lived there with her. For the people who didn't want to eat meat, there were plenty of fruit trees and nuts and other plants that were in season and getting ripe.

The nights had been warm so far and many people preferred to sleep out under the gorgeous pink night sky. It never got really dark and was nicer than being stuck in the passenger bay of the prison transport. Cindy didn't blame them. The bays were kind of creepy.

Cindy knew that the future was uncertain

for them all, however, and had insisted that shelter would come before anything else. Niemand had wanted to call them barracks, but Cindy didn't like that term - it reminded her of the military camp. She called them apartment complexes instead, because it reminded her of her home on Earth. Even though this was her home at the moment, she still wanted to go back to Earth again – one day. Cindy glanced up to see Niemand, Soleil, and Mycia watching her quietly. Her face got warm as she asked what she had just missed.

"You didn't miss anything." Soleil was quick to assure her.

"You just looked like you were thousands of light-years away." Mycia winked at her.

"In a way, I was. I was thinking about a lot of stuff." Cindy said. "Which reminds me, when is the training going to start?"

"Next week." Niemand answered.

"That's good to know. I'd like to take part in the training exercises. I think that everyone should learn how to fight and fly better." Cindy said.

"I agree with Cindy." Mycia nodded slowly as he spoke. "Everyone here should brush up on how to fight with and without weapons." He looked serious. "So they can defend themselves in an emergency."

"But what about those who just want to stay here?" Soleil asked. "Why would they need to know how to fight? This planet is very well protected by the nebula."

"Yes, Havenland is protected, but what happens if most of us are away and our enemies figure out how to get past the nebula?" Cindy replied with a questioning glance.

"Ahhh…" Soleil said with a grin. "If you and others are gone, the rest of us can stay here and beat anyone up who isn't supposed to be here!"

"Yep." Cindy winked at him. "Unless there is anything else that needs to be discussed, let's get back to work."

With a couple shakes of their heads, the little group broke up. Cindy didn't have anything that she had to do for a while, so she headed out to the waterfall, following the rim of the lake.

So much had happened to her in the last few months. She remembered her home on Earth, but she didn't feel as homesick as she used to. Havenland was her home now and she knew that the people with her were counting on her to be a good leader. They were becoming her new family.

Mycia, Niemand, Wishter, and Soleil were

all big helpers in trying to keep the group reassured and safe. Daruka and Michella were great at counseling the women and children about how things were going as well as leading them in collecting food to keep everyone fed through the winter.

Mycia and Wishter were in charge of building the apartments while Soleil was in charge of the groups that went out to get timber for the apartments. Niemand was keeping track of everything and had kept a close eye on her.

Cindy couldn't really figure out why Niemand watched over her so closely, but she was glad that he did. Niemand was very good at being there without making it obvious. Because of how he handled it, she was able to safely roam without feeling confined or even watched.

Cindy looked around her and smiled. The trees were a beautiful emerald green and the sky was an amazing shade of swirling cloudlike pinky purple that continuously changed shapes. As she looked out across the lake, she heard a deep snarling noise behind her. She could feel the hair on the back of her neck stand on end as she slowly turned around to see a big ape-like creature staring at her. The creature, standing over seven feet tall, was covered in a mottled green and brown shaggy fur - its hands and feet were tipped with long sharp nails. It's mouth contained yellow brown pointed teeth and a pair of long sharp fangs. Cindy froze. Before she could even think about what to do, Niemand sprang out of the forest behind the creature. Without pausing he fired his stun-gun at close range into its back. He fired again. She watched dumbfounded as the creature was unfazed by the energy blast.

Cindy screamed as the creature turned around and hit Niemand – sending him flying back into the woods. The creature then turned back to Cindy. Still frozen with shock she waited for its next move. The creature leapt over to her, grabbed her wrist, and pulled.

Cindy kicked the creature's leg as hard as she could, taking it by surprise. Perhaps its usual prey was so frightened it didn't fight back. She twisted and jerked her arm free, turned and ran. She could hear the creature's growls and snarls as it pursued her. Up ahead she could see a tree with a hole at the base. A fire had burned an opening into the trunk. She darted inside the small opening and pressed against the tree trunk.

Cindy could see that her pursuer was trying

to figure out where she had gone. It looked beyond the tree and then back at it – its puzzled expression would have made her laugh if she wasn't so scared. As it slipped around the trunk, she breathed a sigh of relief. The creature would surely leave now.

The moment of relief didn't last very long, however, as the creature's hand pulled her out of the crevice. Cindy shook with terror as the giant ape's hand dragged her closer to its snarling mouth. Something deep inside of her stirred as she got even closer to the ape's long teeth.

Suddenly, Cindy just felt like singing a soothing song. She started humming and was surprised that the ape stopped pulling on her. As she kept humming the lullaby, the creature released its hold on her altogether.

Stepping away, Cindy finally spoke after her humming died away in the quiet of the moment. "I don't want to hurt you, but I don't want you to hurt me either." The creature's only response was to turn and walk away.

Cindy watched the ape leave and then collapsed shaking with reaction to the last few minutes. She had never known that she could run so fast or so far. What had just happened? How could she have started to sing, of all things, when it seemed like she was about to be killed and probably eaten? As she caught her breath from the entire ordeal, she glanced around. Nothing around her looked familiar. She couldn't even see the lake. Cindy decided that she could solve the puzzle later – she needed to find Niemand first.

Cindy stood up and started tracking her way back to the point where the initial encounter had happened. The creature's tracks were easy to follow in the damp dirt of the forest. She breathed another sigh of relief when she got back to the lakeside.

Cindy knew that she needed to find Niemand quickly – he might be hurt, so she called out for him. When there was no answer, she started to get worried. Heading into the woods again without tracks to follow back was not her idea of a good time, but since he wasn't answering she knew that Niemand might have been badly hurt.

After a few minutes, Cindy found Niemand lying on his back with one of his legs at a strange angle. "Niemand? Are you okay?" *Stupid question* she thought, but she was just so relieved that he was alive

"No. I'm not okay." Niemand answered through clenched teeth. He thought so to! His eyes opened for a minute to see Cindy's worried face as she kneeled beside him and added gently, "But I'll be fine."

"What should I do?" a very concerned Cindy asked. *Come on, stupid . . . hold yourself together . . . panicking isn't going to help . . . You're supposed to be the leader . . . so lead!* The thoughts tumbled through her mind

"My leg is broken. Can you get help before dark?" Niemand groaned as he tried to sit up without success. "I need you to get Wishter and a couple other men out here."

"Alright." Cindy stood up. "Will you be okay here by yourself?"

"I'll be fine." Niemand responded.

Cindy ran back the way she came until she got to the lake. About a half hour later alternating jogging, walking and running she reached the camp. She stopped for a moment, bent over with hands on her knees to hold herself up getting some breath back. "Wishter!" she shouted.

"I'm here." Wishter responded as he jogged up to her. After looking at her disheveled appearance, came the question, "What happened to you?"

"That doesn't matter. Niemand is hurt and needs help." Cindy gasped out as she fought to catch her breath for the third time that day.

"I need some men here now!" Wishter

yelled and then added, "And bring lights too!" Turning back to Cindy, he asked, "What happened?"

Cindy had recovered enough to tell him the short version of what had happened. "A big creature attacked us. Niemand tried to stun it, but the stun-gun didn't stop it. It hit Niemand and he went flying a couple dozen feet back into the woods. We need to hurry. He is alone out there, it is getting dark, and he is hurt. A lot I think"

The rescue team arrived, carrying the gear they would need and immediately they started to follow as Cindy led them back up her trail. "How bad is Niemand hurt?" Wishter asked, worried about his friend.

"His leg is broken, but there might be more damage than just a broken leg." Cindy answered. She felt guilty that Niemand had gotten hurt. If she hadn't gone for a walk today, none of this would have happened.

Wishter seemed to read her mind and shot her a knowing glance. "It wasn't your fault, Cindy. We are all here under your command and he was just trying to protect you. You couldn't have known that this creature would attack you."

Cindy replied with a sigh. "You're right. I just hope Niemand'll be okay."

"He'll be fine. It is hard to kill someone like him." Wishter winked at Cindy. "In fact, it is hard to kill any of us older guys. Getting killed is the last thing we'll do and that's just too final for us!"

For the first time since the attack, Cindy laughed.

CHAPTER 12

Niemand watched as the sky got darker. He hoped that Cindy had found her way back to the camp and hadn't gotten herself lost. *I shouldn't have sent her back by herself,* he thought *Idiot! I wouldn't have been able to crawl a few feet, never mind travel the distance to the camp! I should've remembered to grab the emergency bag... and the next time that girl leaves camp without a communicator, I'm going to give her a lecture!* At least if Cindy didn't get back by dark, Mycia would organize search parties.

If anything happened to that girl, he would be so mad at himself. He hadn't had the opportunity to tell her his biggest secret. He had planned on telling her by the waterfall, but they hadn't reached it before that creature had attacked.

Niemand wondered how she had escaped from the ape-like creature. He knew that once they caught their prey, well, the prey was usually found as a pile of bones. He didn't know why it had continued to go after Cindy instead of coming after him since he had made it mad. He also needed to remember that a stun-gun doesn't work on the Appelogious. He thought back to the article he had read on the strange creatures. They lived in social groups and were generally quite friendly to humans when in their groups, but when a 'loner' took off from their group, well, they became very dangerous.

After what seemed to Niemand like many more hours than it actually was, the party led by Cindy found him.

"Hey, Niemand, how is it going old friend?" Wishter asked in a cheerful voice.

"Terrible." Niemand growled. "Are you okay, Cindy?"

"Yes, I'm fine." Cindy reassured him quickly.

"Good. Now how much are you going to hurt me this time, Wishter?" Niemand grunted through clenched teeth as Wishter poked and prodded him.

"Not very much more." Wishter grinned. "Your leg is busted pretty badly my friend, we'll need to set it before anything else."

"Great. Just hurry up and get it over with will you?" Niemand growled.

"You heard the man. Hume, hold him down. I'll straighten the leg. If Hume needs help, would you help him, Tom?" Wishter gave directions as he gave Niemand a heavy dose of an immediate painkiller.

"Sure thing, Wishter." Tom replied as Hume took his place holding Niemand's upper body in place.

"What do you want me to do?" Cindy asked, concern written across her face.

"Just being here is enough." Niemand looked right at her with that statement.

Wishter moved into position and with expert ease, pulled the leg straight. Cindy started to cry as she watched and heard Niemand groan in pain. "Cindy, grab those two sticks over there. Hurry!"

Cindy quickly grabbed the two sticks and handed them to him. She watched with unashamed tears streaming down her face as Wishter made a makeshift splint from the sticks and his own shirt.

Niemand was out cold when they were done and Wishter said that it was for the best. "Cindy, Niemand has a couple broken ribs on top of his broken leg. He needs his rest and while he is out cold, he won't be in so much pain."

Cindy merely nodded miserably and watched as the men made a makeshift stretcher to carry Niemand back to camp. As they headed carefully back, no one had much to say about anything.

Later that night, Cindy crawled into her makeshift bed under the sky. She was glad that Niemand would be alright. So very glad. She made a promise that night to be more careful in the future so that she wouldn't be the cause of any more accidents.

When Cindy visited Niemand a few days later, the first thing that popped up was how she got away from the creature. "I don't know for sure. I just remember humming to it and it relaxing. It finally just let me go and walked away."

"You have the gift of talking to animals." Niemand said quietly. "Use your gift well and don't share it with anyone. Every royal child of the Terbiate people has a gift, but they are usually very different from each other."

"Why can't I share it with anyone?" Cindy asked confused.

"Because every gift can be used against you. Some people have learned how to manipulate the gift's powers to control royal blood. Guard your secret well, Cindy."

"How do you know so much?"

"I was your mother's pilot and friend. More than that, I am…" Niemand's sentence was lost in a yell for Cindy.

"Sorry, I got to get over there."

"Don't worry about it." Niemand smiled sadly. Apparently now was not the time to tell Cindy either. "You go do what you need to do to keep this place afloat."

Cindy smiled at Niemand, got up, and then ran over to where Wishter was waiting impatiently. "What's the problem, Wishter?"

Mycia, butting in, spoke like a man hanging onto the shreds of his temper. "The problem is that we need to know what is going on out there and this man won't let me take a ship to find out." Mycia growled as he glared at Wishter.

"It isn't safe out there. We haven't started training people yet." Wishter responded indignantly.

"I have tested a lot of these people and they have already been trained!" Mycia's shout made Cindy jump.

"Okay, that's enough you two." Cindy

said. She paused in thought for a few seconds. "I have to agree with Mycia on this one. We really do need to know what's happening out there, but I also agree with Wishter. Some things still need done around here."

"Then what would you have us do?" The men's murmured question made Cindy step back and think. What was she going to do? She needed to make a wise decision here.

Finally she said, "First, finish the apartments. Then, we will infiltrate the Terbiate and Nythian ranks so that we've got up-to-date intel. Does that sound like a plan?"

Cindy watched as the rest of the men turned to Mycia and Wishter. She could tell that these two men weren't used to being under anyone, let alone a girl, and were having a really hard time deciding if her idea was a good one. They both finally nodded their heads in agreement.

"It's a very good plan." Mycia said, turning to Cindy. He bent his head her direction. "You're a good leader."

Wishter followed suit. "You're a very good leader, Cindy."

"Thank you both." Cindy said, tipping her head towards them. "Now, let's get back to work, shall we?" She grinned as everyone turned back to their work.

Cindy smiled as she walked around the area that was fast becoming organized into a base under the directions of Mycia and Wishter. The men were working together putting the buildings up and it wouldn't be much longer until they were completely finished.

Some of the women had also been very busy. Almost every room had two beds with soft mattresses that they had made from materials that had been found and gathered. The other women had continued their training so that they could also fly. Cindy watched with pleasure as the kids were learning how to happily play again without having to worry as much about what their future would hold. She smiled at the ladies who had taken on the responsibility of watching the children's games to make sure that they didn't get hurt or into trouble.

Every minute of the work the group was putting in was worth it and more Cindy knew. She would have to set up an information network and soon. They urgently needed to know what was happening outside the nebula – in Terbian and Nythiash. The help of Mycia, Wishter, Daruka, Michella, and Niemand would be vital. Soleil had decided that he could best contribute by staying behind on Havenland.

ʚ·ʚ·ʚ·ɞ·ɞ·ɞ

A week later, Mycia, Wishter, Daruka, Michella, and Cindy gathered around an upset Niemand who was still ordered to stay in bed by Wishter. They all agreed that Cindy's idea would work very well. Niemand warned though that "If our people aren't placed in the right situations, they will be caught. No one wants that to happen."

"Well, a few of us are from the Nythian farm districts. We could spread out and be unnoticed while gathering information." Daruka suggested.

"I'd be of more use staying here." Michella said. "I grew up in the military on Nythiash. There is no way that I can sneak back in now and pretend nothing happened."

"I agree with Michella there." Niemand added. "She and I can't just blend in because of who knows us by sight and what we've done. That goes for Mycia as well."

"I am good at sneaking though!" Mycia retorted.

"Yes, you're a great sneak, Mycia." Cindy broke in with a grin. "I think that Daruka and those she feels are qualified should go to the

Nythiash farmlands. Wishter should be able to talk his way back into good graces at the King's Court along with his crew. Mycia should use his sneaking ability to relay messages back and forth until we get a techy system figured out better. Agreed?"

"I agree with Cindy." Niemand was quick to respond. "Her plan's well thought out and it has a pretty good chance at succeeding."

"I think so too." Wishter said as he and Niemand exchanged a knowing glance. "I could always talk my way out of trouble in the King's Court."

"Very true." Niemand grumbled then turned away.

Cindy made a mental note to talk to Niemand about this later as Michella asked, "What do I do, then?"

"We need more pilots trained and I've seen you working with people." Mycia spoke up. "I think you'd be a great teacher."

"That sounds like fun! Can I do that, Cindy?" Michella turned to Cindy.

"I think that's a fabulous idea." Cindy agreed with a smile. "I think that'd work out perfectly."

"In my free time, I can get some of our technology working better if you'd like or even get new technology." Mycia offered with a grin. "I'll just need a few helpers."

"You haven't let me down yet, Mycia, so feel free to ask around for volunteers." Cindy happily said.

"Let's get moving then." Niemand said as Cindy nodded in agreement. He watched as Cindy and Daruka went off together to gather up Daruka's group and to say their farewells. He was so glad that everything seemed to be working out so well. And he was extremely proud of Cindy

As Niemand started to laugh to himself about the worries he had had about Cindy, he winced. His ribs and leg still hurt a lot even though Wishter had said that he would be fine in another two months! Maybe everything working out was a little bit of an exaggeration on his part.

CHAPTER 13

Two months later, Cindy looked up from the latest report from Daruka's pal, Darma, to see Niemand walk into her office. She was glad to see him up and about. "How are you today, Niemand?"

"I'm doing much better now that I'm not in pain." Niemand said with a smile. "How's the network plan working out?"

"Wonderfully!" Cindy said excitedly. "No one even knows who Daruka or anyone else from her party really is and Wishter was able to get off with spending a night in jail."

"Spending a night in jail won't hurt him." Niemand said pulling a silly face. "Are the Terbiates and Nythians still at each other's throats?"

"Unfortunately, yes." Cindy said with a

frown. "Things have gotten so bad that the network has started getting groups ready to evacuate here."

"I didn't realize that things were so bad already." Niemand shook his head. "King Zonien is becoming a fool in his old age."

"Did you know him well?" Cindy asked, curious about what connection to the Royal Family Niemand seemed to be hiding from her.

"No, he never liked me very well." Niemand sighed. "If he had given me a chance, things could have been so very different."

"How could they have been different?" Cindy probed.

Niemand looked at her and then back down. Today was not the time to tell her either. There was too much happening outside the nebula to spring his news on Cindy. "I could have just stayed with my family."

"Oh. I see" . . . *or not!* she thought, but Cindy could see her friend's sadness, so she dropped the subject. She didn't know what to say other than "I miss my family too."

"Yes, I am sure you do, but your family is really…" Niemand was cut off by a shout for Cindy. Again.

"I'm in here." Cindy called.

143

A messenger ran into her office. "Cindy, we have to get our people out of there! The war between the Terbiates and Nythians has started!"

"Niemand, get the crews and their ships prepped. I'll take one of the new ships Mycia got for us to the Terbiate capital on Terbia to evacuate Wishter and his team." Cindy said hurriedly and then turned to the messenger as Niemand ducked out of the room. "Thank you. You look exhausted – go get some rest."

A few minutes later, Cindy was hurrying across the camp to where the ships were parked. Niemand came up beside her. "All of the pilots have been alerted. All except two of the ships have a pilot. We'll pilot one of them."

"No. Your leg and ribs aren't a hundred percent yet and there could be some hairy flying. I need you to pilot *The Canary Dido*. Canary Dido will allow it to pretty much pilot the ship itself." Cindy said firmly. "I'll be fine, but others might not survive if we don't get them off of the planets!"

"Alright, but you be very careful!" Niemand cautioned.

"I will be." Cindy stopped and smiled at him before continuing on her way. "When we all get back, you can tell me what you were going to about my family, okay?"

"Okay."

The next few minutes were spent hurriedly telling the pilots about their pick up locations where they would find their important 'live cargo'. Cindy ended the briefing with these words, "Be careful, fly safe, and come home alive!"

Cindy watched for a moment as everyone rushed off to their ships. How she hoped that everyone would get out alive. How she hoped that the ten ships they now had would have enough room on board to get everyone out in just a couple of trips or less.

Cindy climbed into the *Tradceon* and flipped the radio on. "Is everyone good to go?"

A chorus of voices let her know that everyone was ready. "Then let's make this happen!" Cindy said and flipped the transmitter off. Cindy noticed that all of the ships had been well taken care of by Michella and Soleil as the engine roars sounded just right as everyone started their spacecraft.

Cindy followed the group up into the sky until they hit the edge of the atmosphere. She then gave the *Tradceon* as much fuel as it needed to get up to speed. As the nebula came closer and closer to the line of ships, she turned inertial on and the engines off.

145

Cindy relaxed and tried to enjoy the view through her cockpit window, but thoughts kept spinning around in her head. *What if everyone they were going to try and rescue had already been killed? What had Niemand kept trying to tell her about his past? How dangerous would this mission be? Would anyone be able to find their hidden world?*

Cindy forced herself to relax. She had to do her part – which hopefully would be fairly easy. All she needed to do was land on the private landing pad Wishter had shown her. Once there, she would take onboard about twenty people who would need her to pilot them safely back to Havenland.

The only difficulty that Cindy could think of was getting past the Royal Guard. Since she would be quite close to the palace Royal Guard Traffic Control would be sure to ask for her ship's identification. She hoped that the code Wishter had sent with his last message was up-to-date.

As the *Tradceon* got closer to the outside edge of the nebula, Cindy went in the back to hook up the hyperdrive cables. She counted to a hundred and fifty before plugging the final cables together – she was taking no risks of still being in the nebula. She had no wish to be blown up from the inside out.

Rushing back to her pilot seat, she started the hyperdrive up after fixing her destination into the navigation computer. Sitting back in her chair she thought about everything that had happened since she had been kidnapped by Niemand. She laughed as she realized how long ago that seemed to have been. Once she glanced at the dashboard calendar, however, she realized that she had only been in space for about six months.

Cindy thought back to the birthday celebration her parents had been planning for her seven months ago. There was no way that any party they could have given to her would have been as exciting as being a prisoner under Mia's tutorage. She had told no one about her birthday because it really wasn't on her mind at that time and too much had been happening since.

Cindy was amazed how much her goals had changed in the past months. When she had been taken from Earth, she just wanted to go home. Nothing else had entered her mind except for how to stay alive and how to escape to Earth. Now she didn't even really miss her home on Earth. Maybe someday she would go back, but not anytime soon! The only thing that was pulling her back was her family, but she had come to fully look on her people as her family.

Cindy was also amazed at how much she had learned to do. Mycia, Michella, and Soleil had patiently taught her as much about spaceships as they could while Niemand's leg was still healing. She had learned how to better fly and was taught various tricks that had been passed down through 'The Legends' – those early mercenaries who had written the combat flight manual from scratch! She had faithfully practiced every self-defense technique that had been taught to everyone on Havenland and she could read and speak most of the languages where various members of her people came from.

Her wish on this night was so different from – yet the same as – that first wish in space: to get back home safely and to be with all her friends. Now though, 'home' had changed and she wished for the safety of all the people looking for a safe place to call home and for all of the pilots who were, like her, risking their lives to go into the warzone to rescue them. Tomorrow would be the day to decide many people's fates. Cindy fell asleep in her pilot's seat lulled by watching the stars pass her at incredible speeds.

Cindy woke up as the alarm went off announcing that the *Tradceon* was about ready to come out of hyperdrive. A long-distance communication message popped up on screen and she read that the first few groups of people were safely on Havenland. The *Tradceon* was the slowest ship, so she just had this one stop to make and then it was back home.

The radio crackled to life as a gruff voice said, "Unidentified spacecraft, please identify yourself immediately. This is The Terbiate Royal Guard."

Cindy flipped on her transmitter to say, "This is Francy on the *Trady*. We are here to pick up Wishter and his guests. Our identification code is nine - four - three - eight." She flipped off her transmitter and tensely waited. If the code wasn't good, she would be fired upon. Or toast!

"You are clear to pass. Good day Miss Francy." came the crackled response. Cindy let out a long sigh. She hadn't realized she was holding her breath! She was so glad not to have to fight her way down to the planet's surface to get Wishter and the others.

A short-range coded message from another of her pilots in the area popped up on her screen. She quickly decoded it to read that they were the last pilots in the area. They were wondering if they should wait for her or if she would be fine.

Cindy replied that she would be okay and to go ahead and get safely home. The reply back brought a smile to her face. It read: "Good luck, Cindy! Come home safely! If you need anything, *The Canary Dido* will be arriving in about twenty minutes." She watched her long range scanners as her fellow ship jumped into hyperspace.

Cindy carefully guided her ship down onto the pad that Wishter had directed her to use. As soon as she lowered the steps so that they could get on board, she heard them clambering up the steps. A girl about her own age was between Wishter and another man, both hooded so she couldn't see their faces.

"Who is she?" Cindy asked puzzled.

"Not now, Cindy. Get us out of here! We have guards after us!" Wishter exclaimed in a rather panicked voice.

"Is everyone on board?" Cindy quickly asked. Once Wishter let her know that there weren't any other friendlies coming, she lifted the steps and smoothly fed power into the engines. To save precious seconds she had kept them running on low power. As the her ship lifted off, she could see members of the royal guard shooting at her. Precious seconds indeed!

The *Tradceon* was a small craft and packed with people. Cindy knew that she would have to act fast to get them out of there alive. Although the guard's firepower wasn't anything compared with the ship's, she knew they would soon be in pursuit.

"Would you mind telling me why they are after us, Wishter?" Cindy growled as she expertly avoided the missile that narrowly missed one wing.

"They are after us, because this here," Wishter motioned to the girl, "is Princess Annalise."

"You brought the Princess of the Terbiate people on board?! Are you crazy, Wishter?!" Cindy couldn't help but scream at him. "She's the one who locked us up!"

"And the mysterious person who let you free." Princess Annalise yelled back. "I wanted to come and my grandfather here needed to be rescued from the scoundrel who calls himself the Nythian President."

Cindy just groaned. Now she had the King and, in fact, both the Princesses of the Terbiate people on board. If President Koduko had any sense, he would have alerted

The Royal Guard that King Zonien had been kidnapped by the ship she was flying! How would she get out of this situation?

CHAPTER 14

"I had to help them, Cindy." Wishter said. "King Zonien has been under lock and key for months now. He has been forced to do whatever President Koduko wants him to. The war was made to stage his death."

"Well, it would've been a good way to take over for good." Cindy growled. "But now what am I supposed to do? We have enemy fighters on our six!"

"Maybe I could try talking sense into them?" King Zonien suggested wearily.

"I'm afraid that won't work." Cindy said without giving him a glance. "The last message given to all pilots was that we've killed you and we have voice synthesizers to make it sound like you're talking."

"That's just wonderful!" Princess Annalise

growled.

Cindy watched her scanner as they climbed higher into the atmosphere. They were almost to the hyperspace jump point when one fighter hurtled past the *Tradceon* firing all available weapons. She heard the engines whine down to a stop as the damage meter blazed red in the dark cabin.

"Cindy! The engines have stalled! We've taken heavy damage. We're in no shape to make a soft landing . . . What are you going to do?" Wishter yelled over the explosions coming from the various systems getting fried around them.

Cindy thought quickly. All the other refugees were safely away. They were the last ones left on the battlefield who weren't actually on either side but were hated by both. Flipping the radio switch on, she quickly spoke. "Calling Niemand on *The Canary Dido,* do you copy?"

"Niemand is busy replacing some wiring that got knocked loose, Commander Cindy. Shall I get him for you?" The calm reply from Canary Dido sounded like music to Cindy's ears.

"Canary Dido, there is no time to explain. Beam out my people now and take them to the base! Make sure Niemand gets them safely home and tell him not to worry – I'll be right behind you!" Cindy ordered.

"Yes, ma'am." Canary Dido replied as it began beaming Cindy's crew and passengers away. "What about you? I don't have enough room to take you on board too."

"I'll be fine! Now go!" Cindy yelled into the radio as the last passenger was beamed to safety.

"Are you sure, Cindy?" Canary Dido asked once more.

"Get out of here!" Cindy ordered and watched as the scanner system registered *The Canary Dido* leaving.

Cindy flipped the emergency restart toggle over and over. She was almost to the ground, beginning to think that it was all over when the engines stuttered back to life and then kicked in with a roar. They finally started to level out. She pulled the nose up as hard as she could but it was too late - the *Tradceon* ploughed into the ground throwing up a sheet of soil and debris. Cindy lost consciousness as she was slammed against the instrument panel.

Back on Havenland, Niemand went ship to

ship, checking that everyone was okay. In the rush of their escape, Canary Dido hadn't told him that King Zonien and Princess Annalise were on board or that Cindy was in trouble. All the other ships were back safely - except for the *Tradceon*.

He couldn't stop fretting about Cindy. He could just feel that something wasn't right. He should never have allowed her to go out into the war zone like that. Deep inside Niemand knew better though. He knew that Cindy would have never taken 'no' for an answer. She had too much of her mother and her father in her for that to have happened. Truthfully, he wouldn't have wanted it any other way, but he still wished that he could have told her his secret before this had happened.

Niemand strained to hear the roar of engines before anyone saw the ship approaching. The sky was silent! He prayed that the *Tradceon* was safe and nearly home. Soleil notified him that Canary Dido had requested that he get back on board as soon as the other passengers had gotten disembarked.

"Why?" Niemand asked confused.

Soleil answered. "It's picked up information through the relay satellite system

– there's been a . . ." He hesitated, looking grim ". . . a disaster." Again he paused trying to find an easy way to break the news. "Cindy is still out there all alone and probably hurt. Canary Dido said to notify only you. It wants to take you back to rescue her and *The Canary Dido* is the ship with the best hyperdrive. Mycia had it changed out last month so that it could come and go from Terbia within a couple of hours."

"Alright. I'm on my way." Niemand said with a shaky voice as he sprinted towards the ship. His Princess was out there somewhere. She was in danger, probably hurt, and people were no doubt looking for her. If they found her, it would be a summary execution. More than that, well… he just had to find her.

"Do you want any of us to come with you?" Soleil asked.

"No. I'm leaving Mycia in charge." Niemand said sharply. "I'll be back with Cindy very soon. If I don't get back within two days, assume we're both dead."

"We'll come looking for you." Soleil insisted.

"No! Don't bother. If I am not back within a couple of days, I won't be coming back." Niemand growled. "They aren't going to want to risk losing me again. If I'm caught,

I'm dead!"

Soleil shivered, but nodded in agreement. "Be careful, Niemand."

Niemand merely nodded back and ran up the steps into *The Canary Dido.*

"It is good to see that you got my message Niemand." Canary Dido said. "Hurry up and strap in. I am getting ready to take off again."

Niemand did as he was told because his thoughts were in a whorl and he knew that Canary Dido was programmed to protect its Commander in an emergency. That programming was with or without thought for anyone else - unless of course the Commander overrode it. He was actually surprised that Canary Dido had let him come on board.

Everything was quiet for about an hour as *The Canary Dido* sped back to Terbian. Finally Niemand asked, "Why did you let me come?"

"Two reasons. One is that Cindy might be too injured for me to safely beam her up. The other is because of your relationship to her." The synthetic voice rattled off.

"You know my secret?" Niemand whispered.

"It's a wonder everyone doesn't know. You've been awfully protective of her."

"She's my Commander... and anyway,

everyone on Havenland is protective of her." Niemand argued, not wanting to admit what he hadn't been allowed to admit in over fifteen years.

"That may be, but no one is more protective than a dad and a single parent at that. She has your determination and her mother's loving heart."

"Yes, she does." Niemand whispered as the tears started rolling down his face. "I wish I could've told her that she was my daughter, but the time never seemed to be right."

"Sometimes, you just have to make the time right." Canary Dido replied quietly and then left Niemand to himself for the next hour of the trip.

Back on Terbia, President Koduko was making a public speech over the radio. "My friends of Terbiate, I would like to express my sorrow at the kidnapping and loss of King Zonien and Princess Annalise. We have shot down the spacecraft responsible, but it appeared that everyone had beamed out into another craft. We will do everything it takes to find those evil people and bring them to swift justice. In the meantime, I am willing to stay here as your new ruler until another member of the royal blood is found."

Niemand heard it come over the radio as *The Canary Dido* came out of hyperspace. He just shook his head at the foolishness of the situation. It was likely that President Koduko had King Zonien and Princess Annalise hidden away somewhere, but Canary Dido's next words shocked him. "Princess Annalise and King Zonien are both safely on Havenland. We brought them back. I'm sorry I didn't mention it before but –"

"What?!" Niemand said astonished. "They hate me. Annalise thinks I killed her mother and her sister. She didn't even recognize Cindy when we landed!"

"That might be, but I think that the truth needs to come out sometime. Now, hang on. We are going down." Canary Dido's words were immediately followed by an abrupt, dangerous entry into the atmosphere.

Niemand watched as the gauges blinked red in warning as they quickly approached the ground near the wreck of the *Tradceon*. As the ship settled, Niemand raced down the still lowering steps and out onto the dusty surface.

Niemand ran over to the wreck and then slowed down enough to look it over. It was obvious that the ship had hit hard and fast. The nose was half buried in the churned up ground and the whole ship tilted about twenty degrees to its port side, covering the airlock hatch. He needed to find the safest way to get inside of the *Tradceon*. Or even, at least, hazardous one! No way in through the entry hatch, but the cockpit canopy was near the ground. Noticing that the cockpit window had a large crack in it, he picked up a rock and threw it at the window with all of his might. The rock's impact lengthened the crack and, after a few more hits, it shattered. He used another rock to clear the sharp shards from around the frame. Once most of the glass-like material had gone, he scrambled through the frame into the cockpit and quickly into main chamber.

Niemand let his eyes adjust to the gloom. Once he could see, he found Cindy's body lying halfway on the floor and halfway on the opposite wall. "Oh no." he breathed. Half stepping, half sliding down that slanted floor to her side, he gently reached out and touched her.

Cindy felt someone next to her through the fog that was clouding her mind. She hurt all over, but her head was pounding the most. She tried to say something, but couldn't. All that came out was a soft moan before all went dark again.

Niemand was so relieved when he heard Cindy's moan – she was alive! "I'm here, Cindy. You'll be alright now." He carefully slid his arms under her legs and back. He hoped that he wouldn't hurt her even more as he lifted her. Carefully navigating his way out of the wreckage wasn't easy, but a few minutes later he was carrying his precious daughter up the steps into *The Canary Dido's* cabin.

Canary Dido let down the emergency cot that was normally folded up into the wall. Niemand laid Cindy down and then asked, "Is she going to be okay?"

"I don't know. She needs a mediscan to check the extent of the damage. The mediscanner's were damaged and Mycia didn't have time to fix them." Canary Dido paused. "On the other hand, if you look at the radar scanner you will see that we will have company in approximately seven minutes."

"Then get us out of here. I'll stay with Cindy just in case she wakes up." Niemand growled.

"Yes, sir!" *The Canary Dido's* engines started and the ship accelerated steeply away from the ground.

CHAPTER 15

"Please be very careful." Niemand said. "I don't want a rough ride for Cindy."

"I am going as smoothly as I can." Canary Dido responded, expertly dodging another missile. "We will reach the edge of the atmosphere in five minutes fourteen seconds. I already have the coordinates for Jalamush entered in the navigation computer."

"Good." came Niemand's terse reply before checking Cindy over more closely. He couldn't tell if there was any internal bleeding, but his heart sank when he noticed the gash on her head. It wasn't particularly big and it wasn't bleeding, but it looked like Cindy had collided with the edge of something hard and sharp.

Niemand pulled out the first aid kit and

bandaged Cindy's head. A couple of her ribs were broken, as well as her left arm. He gave her a shot of a powerful painkiller before carefully straightening and splinting her arm. Her ribs would have to wait. *The Canary Dido* didn't have the facilities to let him deal with them. He took some relief in the fact that at least her breathing was regular, though too shallow.

Niemand also checked to see if either of Cindy's legs had been broken, but they were fine. The multitude of bruises, cuts, and minor scrapes he cleaned up as well as he could. He was mostly worried about the gash on her head. That gash was not good news at all.

Niemand felt the hyperdrive kick in and relaxed a little. At least they were out of danger's way as far as being shot down was concerned. He leaned back against the wall of the ship. He didn't even notice that he was drifting off to sleep.

Niemand woke up an hour later as *The Canary Dido* dropped out of hyperspace. He couldn't believe that he had fallen asleep, but he knew that he had been awake for over twenty four hours trying to get people safely to Havenland. "Are we almost home?" He asked sleepily.

"Yes, we are almost home." Canary Dido answered quietly. "How is the Commander?"

Niemand quickly turned towards Cindy. He relaxed as he saw her breathing was still regular and, perhaps, less shallow. She didn't seem any worse. "She's breathing, but still asleep."

"It is good that she is still breathing, but shouldn't she have woken up by now?" Canary Dido asked.

"I don't know. She has a really bad head wound." Niemand sounded worried. "How soon until we land?"

"We will land in about thirty minutes. I will radio ahead and let them know that we are coming in safely." Canary Dido responded.

"That will be good." Niemand quietly said before turning his attention back to Cindy. He checked her wounds and found them to have stopped bleeding, but the swelling on her head was even worse. "I promise you, Cindy, that if you will wake up that I'll be the father that I never had the chance to be." The tears fell from his eyes as he gently touched her face with his hand.

෨෨෨෨෨෨෨

Half an hour later, *The Canary Dido* landed and Niemand called out the doorway to the waiting people. "Where's the stretcher and our doctor? Cindy's very badly hurt." Mycia and Wishter hurried on board with a stretcher and Niemand helped move Cindy carefully onto it. They gently carried her down the steps and into one of the newly completed buildings.

"How bad is she?" The doctor asked as he came hurrying into the room.

Niemand looked the new medic over before answering. He surmised that he was from the farmers on the Nythian planet, Nythea, by his accent and clothes. "Cindy's left arm is broken, along with a couple of her ribs. She has a big gash on her head too. I don't know about internal bleeding though."

The doctor nodded before getting to work. After doing a full examination, he motioned Niemand, Mycia, and Wishter into the adjoining room. "Cindy has some internal bleeding, but the most serious thing is the head wound. I can't do anything more for her other than to make her comfortable while she is still with us. I am sorry, but I don't have any of the proper facilities to perform the required surgery."

Niemand put his face in his hands and looked down, unmoving.

"How long until she . . . dies?" Mycia finally asked.

"I can't give an exact time. It's a miracle that she has hung on this long." The doctor replied.

"So there is a chance that she'll recover?" Niemand asked with tears in his eyes.

"Not unless she gets proper surgery. The swelling on her head will eventually put too much pressure on her brain. That amount of pressure will be enough to kill her." the doctor said with a sad expression. "I'd do it if I could, but I'm not even that skilled with head wounds."

Mycia swung around and hit the wall. "She can't just die!" he growled out while tears glistened in his eyes.

"I don't see there is any choice." Wishter said sadly.

At this point, Niemand looked up. He said determinedly, "I'm taking Cindy back to Earth. She will be able to get the help there that she needs to survive, and it's the only place that we know of where her life won't be in danger."

"It isn't your choice." Michella interrupted him as she and Daruka came through the door. "We came as soon as we heard."

"That's right. It's everyone's choice." Mycia agreed.

"No, it is my choice, because I am her father." Niemand said and then strode out into the other room. "If you don't believe me, then ask King Zonien."

Niemand stopped, fought to get himself back under control, then turned back towards the group and saw them just staring at him.

"You were the father that no one could find?" Wishter finally asked.

"Yeah. King Zonien didn't want me to marry Princess Deborah, but she and I fell in love. We agreed to go ahead and get married. King Zonien found out after our wedding night and had the marriage annulled." Niemand paused and then continued. "No one was supposed to know. Princess Deborah was with child, however, so King Zonien had a marriage license drawn up with a name that no one knew. The story was that he married the Princess and then disappeared."

"You were okay with that?" Mycia skeptically asked.

"No, I was not happy with that!"

Niemand's tone was icy. He took a deep breath and slowly released it. "I didn't have a choice. Deborah made sure that I could still be with her as her pilot and confidante." Niemand said.

"I don't know about you guys, but I believe Niemand." Wishter spoke up. "I think that this is Niemand's choice."

"Agreed." Daruka spoke up. "Besides, I think that whatever can be done to save Cindy should be done."

"I'll tune up the hyperdrive on *The Canary Dido* to help you get back to Earth faster." Mycia said and quickly left.

Niemand breathed a "thank you" and then sat down on a stool beside Cindy. Michella and Daruka both held Cindy's hand for a moment. Then, Michella gently squeezed Niemand's shoulder. "I'm sorry . . . we didn't know . . . please forgive me." she said softly before quietly following Daruka out.

Wishter sat down next to Niemand. "I'll come with you if you'd like me too. I think it would be good for you to have some company - and I still am your best friend."

"Thank you … that would be good." Niemand consented.

A short while later, everything was ready to go. Niemand and Wishter carried the stretcher through the crowd of people who bade a still unconscious Cindy a safe trip with wishes for her to get better and return soon. Everyone cared a lot for Cindy - even those who never had had the chance to get to know her very well. They all knew that she had been hurt while trying to get them out of danger and to safety.

King Zonien and Princess Annalise waited at the foot of the steps of *The Canary Dido* under Mycia's watchful gaze. "Everything is ready." Mycia said in response to Niemand's questioning glance.

Niemand nodded and turned to Princess Annalise. Before he could say anything, she just hugged him. "I'll be here waiting when you get back."

"I'm glad." Niemand said with tears in his eyes. "King Zonien…"

The King interrupted him. "I was wrong to do what I did. I hope you come back safely and I hope that Cindy will be okay. No one should lose a child."

Niemand just nodded and climbed the steps. Canary Dido shut the door as Wishter and Niemand strapped the stretcher down to the cot. As *The Canary Dido* rose into the atmosphere, Wishter patted Niemand's back. "I'll take first watch. You look exhausted.

Get some rest."

Niemand merely nodded and, with one last look at Cindy's face, laid down on the cool floor. He was almost instantly asleep.

❧❧❧❧❧❧

Fifteen hours later, Niemand shook Wishter awake. "We're here."

As Niemand started to say goodbye to the unconscious Cindy, Wishter scanned Earth's surface and found the closest military base to where Niemand had first captured Cindy. He set a marker to beam her down in the middle of what appeared to be an occupied meeting room. *That should get their attention and rapid help for Cindy*, he thought

"The transporter's ready, Niemand. The location that I've chosen should get her immediate help." Wishter said.

"Alright, I'll let you say goodbye to her I'd like to handle the transporter myself." Niemand said.

"Goodbye, Cindy. I hope to see you again one day, sweet girl." Wishter said and, with final squeeze of her hand, he walked away into the engine room with tears streaming down his face.

Niemand pulled Cindy into a gentle hug

and kissed her on the cheek. "May God be with you, my child." He said as he laid her back down. Standing up and walking over to the controls was the hardest thing he had ever done - or so he thought. Closing his eyes, he jabbed where he knew the transporter button was.

As Niemand heard the sound of the beam, he cried out with a sobbing voice, "No!" and sank down on the floor. He hadn't known that it would hurt this much to lose Cindy.

Wishter rushed to Niemand's side and did his best to comfort him. "Let's go Canary Dido." Wishter said as he tried to calm Niemand down. Canary Dido scanned the area. "I'm picking up a great deal of activity. What appear to be medical vehicles are moving towards the building at high speed and there is a great deal of movement in the building and especially inside the room. I think that it is safe to say, Cindy is receiving the help she requires."

The Canary Dido jumped back into hyperspace, heading back for Jalamush.

ᡣᡂᡣᡂᡣᡂᡣᡂᡣᡂᡣᡂ

On Earth, the Commander was having a meeting with his superiors about the disappearance of the alien child registered as Cindy D. Cooper. The meeting wasn't going well for the Commander and Doctor White until a bright white beam flashed and Cindy appeared on their table.

The Commander was shocked. He quickly recovered and took one look at Cindy's bandages and yelled "Get a medical team in here immediately!"

As soon as Cindy had been moved into the operating room, the Commander's superiors packed up. Their last words to the Commander were, "You'd better think up a really good story when you return Cindy to her foster parents."

After the surgery, the Commander and Doctor White called Mr. and Mrs. Cooper with the news that Cindy had been found. "It appears as if she ran away from home and got caught in an experimental explosion here at the base. She's just getting out of surgery and should be fine." Doctor White explained.

"No, she didn't just run away." Mrs. Cooper growled over the phone. "What really happened to my daughter?"

"We don't know." Doctor White said after a pause. "We just don't know."

EPILOGUE

Cindy's eyes fluttered open for an instant before she jumped out of bed. She stared around the room for a few moments before she remembered what had happened. She was back at home at last!

Cindy didn't remember much about the accident, but everybody told her that she had stumbled upon a secret military project at the exact moment that the project had set off an explosion. She just remembered falling and then slipping into unconsciousness. The army personnel had finally left her alone after quizzing her several times about what she remembered.

Cindy lay back down – she still tired quickly, even though she had been at the hospital for several months. She sighed. It felt good to be home again, but she didn't like not being able to remember what had happened at the accident.

Cindy heard a knock on her bedroom door. She immediately pretended to be asleep. She wasn't sure why – something just didn't feel right. She heard the door slowly open and heard someone walking across the room. When the person was almost to her bed she jumped up ready to defend herself against any unknown danger.

One look at her Mom's face and Cindy knew that she was going to head back to the hospital. An automatic self-defense response wasn't supposed to be part of any child's life – especially in their own home and just out of the hospital.

"Are you okay?" Cindy's Mom asked soothingly.

"Yeah, I'm fine. You just scared me." Cindy said relaxing and sitting down on the edge of her bed.

"I know, but you heard the Doctor. If you get scared and react like that, you have to go back to the hospital. That explosion must have shattered your nerves completely. Where did you learn how to just jump up and be ready to fight like that though?"

"I don't remember." Cindy said honestly.

"Please don't make me go back there though. I hate it and I can't even think there. The doctors kind of scare me."

"I know, sweetie, but 'Doctor's Orders' must be followed." Cindy's Mom smiled reassuringly at her. "Come on, let's get ready to go. The sooner we get there, the sooner we can get back home, right?"

"I suppose." Cindy mumbled and watched her Mom walk back out her door. She hated the thought of going back to the hospital.

Cindy grabbed her bag – it was still packed from getting home just last night. Sighing, she thought, *What a long stay at home… Not!* She quickly walked through the quiet house and got into the car.

As Cindy got into the vehicle, she kept thinking, *Maybe, just maybe, the Doctor will just let me come back home.* In her heart, she knew that that was just wishful thinking on her part.

❧❧❧❧❧❧

At the hospital, Cindy was distractedly listening to her Mom and Doctor White. As they began moving away from her, she listened more closely.

"I don't think that it is a good idea for her to be put into a full-time mental hospital."

Cindy's Mom said.

"We both know that she isn't like other kids. We don't know what she is capable of." Doctor White insisted. "This would be safer for everyone."

"She is my daughter. I'll talk it over with my husband, but I think that we will be keeping her with us."

Cindy felt good that her Mom wasn't going to lock her up. She knew that there was a good reason she never had liked Doctor White. He just wanted to lock her up and do tests on her it sounded like. What did he mean when he said that she wasn't like other kids?

The next words that Doctor White spoke sent chills down Cindy's spine. "It may not be up to you any longer Mrs. Cooper. That girl might be a threat to society and the Army has authorized me to remove the threat whenever I deem it necessary and by whatever means necessary."

Cindy liked where Doctor White was going with this even less now. She cautiously looked around, scanning everyone inside the room. She was trying to figure out who would be a threat to her. Suddenly, she realized that all of the so-called patients around her kept watching her with the same gaze that the Commander used.

Cindy didn't know how she could tell that they were all actually military, but she could. She knew that if she didn't get out of here - and now - the decision would not be up to her Mom. She spied her one method of escape. A window was open.

Cindy wasn't sure if she would get hurt by jumping through it. It didn't matter though – she needed an exit and that was the only one available. She nonchalantly went over and looked out of the window. She judged that it wasn't more than seven feet down.

Turning back, she saw the Doctor grab her Mom's arm and raise his voice. "Cindy is staying here until further notice."

Cindy could see that the 'patients' were closing in on her. She made a fast decision and yelled "I love you, Mom!" before spinning around and running back at the window. She dived through it, expertly rolling as she hit the ground, and came out of the roll running fast. *Where ever did I learn to do that?* she thought as she instinctively headed towards the cover of the trees fifty yards away.

Mrs. Cooper and Doctor White watched helplessly as Cindy jumped. When one of the disguised soldiers got to the window, he called back "She's gone."

Mrs. Cooper was held in a small room, alone, for a couple of hours. Her thoughts were whirling around. Finally, Dr. White entered the room. He looked at her coldly. "You are free to go, but you will be watched. If Cindy is found, she will be forcibly returned here."

Mrs. Cooper just glared at the Doctor before spinning on her heel and walking away. She would talk to her husband about this and see if they could get Cindy back into their custody. In the meantime, she hoped that that her little girl had enough sense to not let herself be tracked wherever she went. Maybe, one day, she could come home; but Mrs. Cooper hoped that Cindy wouldn't show up back there just yet.

❧❧❧❧❧❧

Cindy didn't stop running until she made it back into town. As soon as she reached the main street, she started hitchhiking. She knew she would have to get as far away as possible before Doctor White issued a warning notice.

A car driven by a friendly lady picked Cindy up and took her to the next town. Cindy had lied to her and said that she had missed the bus. She didn't feel good about it, but she needed to get away from her previous life. She was still trying to work out what was happening to her and why.

Cindy did the same thing a few more times until she was in a city hundreds of miles away. She couldn't believe that she had made it as far as she had. She suddenly realized that she was miles from home and had no food, no money and no luggage. Not good! Finally, in the early morning hours, with no other viable options, she asked a young man for the bus fare. "I really need the twenty dollars for a bus ticket." Cindy said desperately.

"Why?" The man who was in his early twenties asked.

"I just need to get far away from here. A hospital was going to take me away from my parents." Cindy risked the truth with tears pooling in her eyes.

"I'll help you, don't worry." the man said. "My name is David Liteon and I might even have a place for you to stay."

"Really?" Cindy got a hopeful look in her eye. "Where?"

"With me." David said. He laughed at Cindy's horrified expression. "I live with my grandparents. I'm not a bad person who will hurt you."

"Alright. My name is Cindy." Cindy decided to trust this guy since she had no one else.

"Are you hungry, Cindy?" David asked.

"Yes." Cindy answered with a smile. She hadn't eaten in the last fifteen hours.

"Alright, let's go grab some early breakfast before our bus gets here."

Over breakfast, Cindy grew more comfortable with David. He was a nice guy who had just spent two years in college. He was going home because his grandparents needed some help.

Their bus finally arrived and David explained to the slightly suspicious ticket agent that Cindy was his sister. When asked, she agreed with his story. They arrived in David's home town around noon. Cindy had slept most of the way.

"Wake up, sleepyhead." David said as he poked Cindy in the ribs. Cindy woke up with a start. "Sorry, didn't mean to startle you."

"It's okay." Cindy yawned and scrambled to follow David across the street towards an older gentleman. David greeted the man warmly and hugged him. Cindy let David explain her situation to his grandfather and was surprised as his grandfather pulled her into a hug too.

When they all got to David's grandparents' house, Cindy was bemused that his grandmother was even more glad to see her than his grandfather had been. After a nice, warm meal, Cindy was taken up to the guest room. Mrs. Liteon brought out one of David's mother's nightgowns for Cindy.

Once Cindy was alone, she looked up into the starry night sky. The Liteons had insisted that she would be welcome there for as long as she wanted to stay, but Cindy couldn't help feeling like she belonged somewhere in the space above near one of those bright stars.

One day, Cindy wanted to have a chance to go to space. She didn't know what waited for her there. In the meantime, she would do everything it took to keep herself out of the hospital. She hoped that her Mom and Dad were alright.

Cindy wasn't the only one looking up at the stars. Niemand had become the leader on Havenland and had gotten to know his other daughter very well. King Zonien was back in charge of his Kingdom and President Koduko was more than happy to stay on his side of the border between their two systems as

Niemand had taken his son as a hostage. The truth was that President Koduko's son had been disgusted with his father's actions and had wanted to join the community on Havenland. The President didn't know this, so the bluff worked.

Niemand supposed that he should be happy, but he still missed Cindy's presence. He hoped that she was happy and safe, but he couldn't help feeling a pull back to Earth – a pull that he couldn't answer for at least a few more months, because their people needed his leadership to stay safe until the last bit of hostility died down.

ABOUT THE AUTHOR

Adora Hooper is an imaginative young author who enjoys writing science fiction stories. Time in Space is her opening foray into the possibilities that the genre has to offer. She is currently figuring out what the world has to offer as she just graduated from high school in June 2014 and moved 1,700 miles away from her parents in September 2014. Right now, she currently is employed as a part-time sales associate at a local convenience store as well as holding a side job writing product descriptions for her mom's business. Even through all this, she has found the time to work on the second installment of The Terbiate Legends, Return to Space.